One Deadly Christmas Tree

An Agatha Royale Mystery
Book 5

Ella Andrew

BACKSPACE
PRESS

Copyright © 2025 by Ella Andrew

www.ellaandrew.com

First paperback edition December 2025

Backspace Press

Houston, Texas

Cover design by BACKSPACE PRESS

ISBN 979-8-9932530-9-1 (paperback)

ISBN 979-8-9932530-8-4 (ebook)

Printed in the United States of America

Chapter 1

A Festive Beginning

The scent of pine filled One Deadly Chapter Books & Brew as Agatha Royale balanced precariously on the stepladder, reaching to drape a garland across the top of the cozy mystery section. Below her, Mike sat at attention, his salt-and-pepper coat illuminated by the soft glow of the café lights, his tail wagging as he supervised.

"A little to the left," Emma called from the café counter, where she was arranging a display of Christmas-themed mysteries.

Agatha adjusted the garland, tucking a sprig of holly into the pine boughs. "Better?"

"Perfect! Very Dickensian."

"Mon Dieu, be careful up there!" Lorraine swept through the front door in a flurry of snowflakes and dramatic gestures, her purple coat dusted with white. "We cannot have our famous detective falling and breaking her neck before the tree lighting ceremony!"

Agatha climbed down carefully, brushing pine needles from her sweater. She'd learned to take Lorraine's pronouncements with a grain of salt, though the older woman's theatrical flair never failed to make her smile. "I'm hardly famous, Lorraine."

"Psh!" Lorraine waved this away, unwinding her scarf with a flourish. "You catch killers the way some people catch colds! The whole town speaks of you with respect, ma chérie."

Emma grinned, pushing her tortoiseshell glasses up her nose. "She's not wrong. You're basically Bristol Lake's resident Sherlock Holmes."

"I prefer Miss Marple," Agatha said.

"Oui, but Miss Marple, she did not have murders fall at her feet quite so often!" Lorraine gestured dramatically. "Everywhere you go, ma chérie—poof! Another body, another mystery. C'est incroyable!"

"That's not exactly comforting, Lorraine."

Mike barked, as if in agreement, then trotted over to investigate a box of ornaments Lorraine had set on the floor.

"Non, non, petit chien!" Lorraine scooped up the box before Mike could knock it over. "These are for the tree, not for your archaeological excavations."

Agatha laughed, scooping Mike into her arms. He licked her chin enthusiastically. "He just wants to help."

"He wants to cause chaos," Emma corrected, but her tone was fond. She'd been Agatha's best friend since those early days, and Mike had won her over completely despite his tendency to dig up evidence—and occasionally, inconvenient flowerbeds.

The bookstore had evolved beautifully over the past few years. The café still served Eliza's baked goods, the Christie Corner remained a favorite spot for customers, and the hidden reading nook behind the movable bookshelf had become something of a legend among local book lovers. Now, draped in evergreen and twinkling lights, it felt positively magical.

"So," Agatha said, setting Mike down and surveying their progress, "tell me about this tree lighting ceremony. I've been so busy with the bookstore, I haven't paid much attention to the planning."

"Oh là là, you are missing all the excitement!" Lorraine clasped her hands together. "Bristol Lake is hosting the County Christmas Tree Competition this year. It is très important—judges are coming from all the surrounding towns!"

Emma nodded, carefully hanging a vintage mystery book ornament on the small tree they'd set up near the café. "It's a huge deal. The winning town gets bragging rights for the entire year, plus a fancy plaque and some grant money for community improvements."

"How very festive," Agatha said. "Though I'm detecting a note of something else in your voice, Emma."

"That's because people take it very seriously." Emma made air quotes around the last two words. "Like, *very* seriously. My predecessor at the library still hasn't forgiven Rockland for winning three years ago. Apparently, there were accusations of bribery."

Lorraine gasped dramatically. "Bribery! Over a Christmas tree?"

"People get competitive about the strangest things," Agatha mused, thinking of some situations she'd witnessed in her life. Small-town dynamics could turn deadly over far less. She pushed the thought away. This was Christmas, and she was determined to enjoy the season without suspecting everyone of nefarious motives.

Mike, apparently sensing her mood shift, pressed against her leg. She reached down to scratch behind his ears.

"When is the ceremony?" she asked.

"Tomorrow evening," Emma said. "The tree is already up in the town square—it's gorgeous, a twenty-foot Norway spruce. They've been decorating it all week. Tomorrow the judges will arrive, there'll be carols and hot cider, and then the big tree lighting. Mayor Crawford is giving a speech."

"Dennis Crawford," Lorraine added with a knowing look. "The new mayor. Very handsome, very...how do you say...polished? His wife Rebecca is quite elegant as well."

Agatha noted the slight edge in Lorraine's tone. "But?"

"But nothing!" Lorraine said quickly. "They are fine. Just...perhaps a little too aware of their position, oui? Very concerned with appearances."

Emma and Agatha exchanged glances. Lorraine was the town's unofficial gossip clearinghouse, but she had good instincts about people. If she was being diplomatic, there was probably something worth noting.

"Well," Agatha said, adjusting a string of lights, "I suppose we'll meet them tomorrow at the ceremony. The bookstore will be closed for the evening so we can all attend."

"Celeste is coming too," Emma said. "She's excited. Apparently, Petunia Heights has won the competition twice, so there's some friendly rivalry."

Mike barked suddenly, his attention fixed on the front window. Agatha followed his gaze to see fat snowflakes drifting past the streetlights on Central Avenue. The evening foot traffic had picked up—people bundled in scarves and coats, carrying shopping bags, their breath forming clouds in the cold air.

"It's going to be perfect weather for tomorrow," Emma said softly. "A white Christmas, just like in the movies."

"Oui, très romantique." Lorraine sighed happily. "Though I hope the judges do not let a little snow influence their decision. Bristol Lake deserves to win on merit alone."

Agatha smiled, stepping back to admire their handiwork. The bookstore glowed with warmth and light, evergreen garlands framed the windows, and the small tree near the café twinkled with ornaments shaped like tiny books and magnifying glasses—a gift from Emma last Christmas. Outside, Bristol Lake looked like a postcard, all snow-dusted roofs and glowing windows.

"This is perfect," she said quietly. "Thank you both for helping."

"Of course, ma chérie!" Lorraine embraced her in a cloud of perfume and enthusiasm. "What are friends for?"

Mike chose that moment to sneeze, having gotten too close to the pine garlands, and they all laughed.

As Emma and Lorraine gathered their coats to leave, chattering about what to wear tomorrow and whether Eliza would bring her famous Christmas cookies to the ceremony, Agatha felt a deep sense of contentment. This was her life now—not the disappointed ex-wife in the city, not the laid-off librarian with no prospects, but Agatha Royale, bookstore owner, amateur sleuth, and valued member of the Bristol Lake community.

Tomorrow would be a beautiful evening, full of carols and celebration, neighbors gathering to appreciate something lovely together. Nothing mysterious, nothing dark, just pure holiday joy.

She had no way of knowing, as she locked the door behind her friends and turned off the café lights, that by this time tomorrow night she'd be standing over a body, Mike straining at his leash, and another murder investigation would begin.

But that was tomorrow. Tonight, Bristol Lake glowed with Christmas magic, and all was well.

Chapter 2

The Ceremony Approaches

The town square bustled with activity the following afternoon. Agatha picked her way carefully across the snow-dusted grass, Mike trotting beside her on his leash, his breath forming little puffs in the cold December air. All around them, volunteers hung wreaths, strung lights, and arranged hay bales for seating around the magnificent Norway spruce that dominated the center of the square.

"Agatha! Over here!" Emma waved from near the hot cider station, where she was helping arrange cups and napkins on a long table draped in red-and-green plaid.

Agatha made her way over, nodding greetings to familiar faces. The entire town seemed to have turned out to help with final preparations. Even Gladys was there, directing a group of teenagers hanging garlands with the authority of a retired schoolteacher.

"It's beautiful," Agatha said, taking in the scene. The tree stood at least twenty feet tall, decorated with thousands of white lights and elegant gold and silver ornaments. A large star waited on the ground nearby, ready to be placed at the top once the ceremony began.

"Isn't it?" Emma beamed. "The decorating committee worked for three days straight. Rebecca Crawford oversaw the whole thing."

"Speaking of the Crawfords," a smooth voice said behind them, "I believe I just saw Dennis heading toward the gazebo."

Agatha turned to find Raymond Aguilar, who was in town for the holidays approaching, looking distinguished in a charcoal wool coat. The former attorney had become one of her trusted friends in Bristol Lake, and his calm presence always reassured her.

Raymond smiled. "Dennis is... eager to make a good impression. This ceremony means a great deal to him. Bristol Lake hasn't won the County Christmas Tree Competition in fifteen years."

"Fifteen years!" Emma's eyes widened behind her tortoiseshell glasses. "I didn't realize it had been that long."

"Oh yes. Rockland has won five of the last seven years. It's become something of a sore point." Raymond's tone was diplomatic, but Agatha caught the undercurrent. This wasn't just about a tree—it was about town pride, bragging rights, and apparently, old wounds.

Mike tugged at his leash, wanting to investigate the interesting smells near the cider station. Agatha held firm, though she let him sniff the air appreciatively.

"Let's go meet the mayor," she said.

They found Dennis Crawford near the gazebo, deep in conversation with a woman in an elegant cream-colored coat. He was in his fifties, Agatha guessed, with silver-touched hair and the kind of polished appearance that spoke of careful grooming and expensive tailoring. His wife stood beside him —Rebecca Crawford, slender and poised, her dark hair swept into a chignon beneath a burgundy hat.

"Mayor Crawford, Mrs. Crawford." Agatha approached with a smile. "Everything looks wonderful."

Dennis turned, and his face lit up with a practiced smile that didn't quite reach his eyes. "Ah, Miss Royale. Bristol Lake's very own amateur detective. Rebecca, you remember Mrs. Royale from the bookstore?"

Rebecca's smile was warmer but more reserved. "Of course. I keep meaning to stop by One Deadly Chapter again. It's been too long."

"Please do," Agatha said. "We've expanded the classic mystery section since your last visit."

"I'm sure you have." Dennis's tone held a hint of condescension, as if solving murders was a charming hobby rather than serious investigative work. "Well, we're delighted you'll be attending tonight. It's important that the entire community shows support. The judges will be looking at community spirit as part of their evaluation."

"Of course," Agatha said pleasantly, though she felt Mike's ears perk up. The little schnauzer had excellent instincts about people, and his neutral stance suggested he wasn't sure what to make of Dennis Crawford yet.

"The judges should be arriving within the hour," Rebecca said, glancing at her watch—a delicate gold piece that looked very expensive. "Patricia Anderson from Rockland, Robert Coleman from Oxford Hills, and Marina Hawkins from Camden. They're all very experienced."

"And Paul Chambers from Petunia Heights," Dennis

added, his smile tightening almost imperceptibly. "Though he's running late, apparently."

Something flickered across Rebecca's face—so quickly Agatha almost missed it. Discomfort? Anxiety? But then it was gone, replaced by her gracious smile.

"Paul is always very thorough," Rebecca said quietly. "I'm sure he'll be here soon."

The way she said "thorough" made Agatha's amateur sleuth instincts tingle. There was a story there, clearly, but this wasn't the time to investigate.

"Well, we won't keep you," Agatha said. "I know you must be busy with preparations."

"Yes, terribly busy." Dennis was already looking past her toward someone else who needed his attention. "Do enjoy the ceremony this evening. Seven o'clock sharp."

As they walked away, Emma muttered, "Is it just me, or is he kind of..."

"Arrogant?" Agatha supplied quietly. "A bit. Though Rebecca seems nice enough."

"Did you notice how tense she got when they mentioned Paul Chambers?" Emma's observational skills had sharpened considerably over the years of amateur sleuthing.

"I did. But that's none of our business tonight. We're here to enjoy a tree lighting, not investigate."

"Right. Of course." Emma grinned. "Just a nice, normal, murder-free evening."

Mike barked, as if in agreement, and Agatha laughed despite herself.

They spent the next hour helping with final preparations. Agatha arranged programs on chairs while Mike supervised from a nearby hay bale, his tail wagging whenever someone stopped to pet him. The square gradually transformed into a winter wonderland—lights glowing against the late afternoon sky, the scent of cinnamon and apples wafting from the cider station, evergreen boughs framing the gazebo where the town choir would perform.

Around five o'clock, a sleek sedan pulled up near the town hall, and three people emerged.

"The judges," Emma breathed, nudging Agatha.

The first was a stern-looking woman in her sixties, wearing a severe black coat and carrying a leather portfolio. Patricia Anderson, Agatha guessed. She surveyed the square with a critical eye, making notes on a clipboard.

The second was a jovial-looking man with a round face and salt-and-pepper beard, bundled in a cheerful red scarf. He immediately headed toward Eliza's bakery stand, which had been set up near the cider station. Robert Coleman, clearly a man who appreciated good baking.

The third was a younger woman, perhaps in her forties, with carefully highlighted hair and nervous energy. She kept checking her phone and glancing around as if expecting someone. Marina Hawkins, Agatha surmised.

Dennis and Rebecca materialized almost instantly, all smiles and gracious welcomes. Agatha watched from a distance as introductions were made, hands were shaken, and the judges were offered refreshments before the evening ceremony.

"Still no sign of the fourth judge," Emma observed.

"Paul Chambers," Agatha said. "From Petunia Heights."

"I wonder what's keeping him."

Lorraine appeared beside them in a flurry of purple wool and dramatic gestures. "Mes amies! Is it not magnifique? The tree, the lights, the judges arriving! Though I hear one is missing, non?"

"Paul Chambers hasn't arrived yet," Emma confirmed.

"Ah, Paul." Lorraine's expression turned knowing. "He is always very particular about his judging, that one. Very thorough in his evaluations. Some might say... too thorough."

There was that word again. Thorough.

"Do you know him?" Agatha asked.

"Know him? Non, not personally. But I know of him." Lorraine lowered her voice conspiratorially. "He is the county health inspector, you see. Very strict. Some restaurants have been shut down because of his inspections. And as a judge, he is just as... how do you say... exacting."

Before Agatha could ask more, Gladys approached with her purposeful stride.

"The ceremony begins in two hours," she announced. "The choir needs to rehearse one more time, and someone needs to make sure the electrical connections for the tree lights are secure. Last thing we need is for the tree to stay dark when we throw the switch."

"A dark tree would certainly cost us points with the judges," Emma agreed.

As Gladys marched off to organize the volunteers, Agatha glanced toward the town hall where the judges were still gathered with the Crawfords. Patricia Anderson looked stern as ever, Robert Coleman was eating what appeared to be a Christmas cookie, and Marina Hawkins kept checking her phone. But no Paul Chambers.

Mike whined softly, pressing against Agatha's leg. She looked down to find him staring toward the road, ears alert.

"What is it, boy?"

But Mike just sat down, his expression inscrutable in the way only a dog's could be.

The sun was beginning to set, painting the sky in shades of pink and gold. In two hours, the square would be filled with people, the choir would sing carols, and the magnificent tree would blaze to life.

It would be beautiful, Agatha thought. A perfect Christmas evening in Bristol Lake.

And she had no reason to suspect otherwise.

Chapter 3

Old Wounds

The Bristol Lake Community Center glowed with warmth and light as Agatha stepped through the doors at six o'clock, Mike trotting beside her. The reception area had been transformed for the pre-ceremony gathering—evergreen garlands draped the walls, a Christmas tree sparkled in the corner, and tables laden with refreshments lined one side of the room.

"There you are!" Emma waved from near the punch bowl, where she stood with Lorraine and several other book club members. "We saved you some of Eliza's gingerbread cookies before the judges ate them all."

Agatha smiled, making her way over. The room buzzed with conversation as townspeople mingled with visitors from neighboring communities. She recognized Patricia Anderson holding court near the fireplace, her severe expression softened slightly as she discussed something with Gladys—probably local history, knowing Gladys. Robert Coleman had indeed commandeered a plate of cookies and was chatting amiably with Raymond Aguilar.

"The fourth judge still hasn't arrived?" Agatha asked, accepting a cup of mulled cider from Emma.

"Non, not yet," Lorraine said, leaning in conspiratorially. "Though Dennis keeps checking his watch and looking toward the door. He is très nervous, that one."

Agatha followed Lorraine's gaze. Dennis Crawford stood near the entrance with Rebecca, both dressed impeccably—him in a charcoal suit, her in an elegant forest-green dress. But Dennis's polished smile looked strained, and Rebecca kept twisting the rings on her left hand, a nervous gesture that belied her composed exterior.

Mike settled at Agatha's feet, content to people-watch. She scratched behind his ears absently, her own observational instincts—honed over years of reading mystery novels and watching detective shows—noting the various dynamics in the room. Marina Hawkins stood slightly apart from the other judges, still checking her phone with that same nervous energy from earlier. The other judges seemed relaxed enough, but Marina radiated anxiety.

"Oh là là!" Lorraine suddenly gripped Agatha's arm. "He arrives!"

The door opened, bringing a gust of cold air and snowflakes. A man in his mid-forties stepped inside, stamping snow from his boots. He was average height with sandy brown hair going gray at the temples, dressed in an expensive-looking navy overcoat. His features were pleasant enough—a strong jaw, blue eyes, a confident bearing—but something about his expression made Agatha think of Mike when the schnauzer had decided he didn't trust someone.

Paul Chambers. It had to be.

The room's energy shifted subtly. Robert Coleman

looked up from his cookies and nodded a greeting. Patricia Anderson's stern face remained neutral. But Marina Hawkins went pale, and Dennis Crawford's jaw visibly tightened.

"Paul," Dennis said, his voice carefully controlled as he crossed to the door. "We were beginning to worry."

"Traffic," Paul said shortly, unbuttoning his coat. His tone was clipped, professional, but not particularly warm. "The roads from Petunia Heights are a mess."

"Of course." Dennis's smile looked painful. "Let me introduce you to some of our committee members—"

"I know the routine, Dennis." Paul's interruption was smooth but unmistakably dismissive. He handed his coat to a nearby volunteer without looking at her, his attention already scanning the room. When his gaze landed on Rebecca, something cold flickered across his face.

Rebecca had gone very still, her hand frozen mid-twist around her rings. The color had drained from her cheeks.

"Rebecca," Paul said, his voice flat. Not hostile exactly, but devoid of any warmth or courtesy. It was the tone one might use when acknowledging a stranger.

"Paul." Rebecca's response was equally icy, each letter precisely enunciated. She didn't move from her position, didn't extend a hand in greeting. The air between them practically crystallized.

Mike whined softly at Agatha's feet. She glanced down to see his ears had flattened against his head, his body tense. He was staring at Paul Chambers with unmistakable distrust.

"Well," Dennis said with forced brightness, "shall we get you some refreshments, Paul? Eliza's bakery has provided some excellent—"

"I'm fine." Paul's dismissal was complete. He moved past Dennis as if the mayor were simply part of the furniture, heading toward where the other judges had gathered.

The snub was deliberate and obvious. A muscle jumped in Dennis's jaw, but he maintained his composed expression, though his hands had curled into fists at his sides.

Emma leaned close to Agatha, whispering, "Did you see that? That was..."

"Hostile," Agatha murmured back. "Definitely hostile."

"There is history there, ma chérie," Lorraine hissed, her eyes gleaming with the thrill of gossip. "Very bad history, I think."

Agatha watched as Paul joined the other judges. His demeanor transformed instantly—warm smile, jovial hand-shake with Robert, respectful nod to Patricia, even a some-what stiff but polite greeting to the nervous Marina. He was charming, she realized. Or at least, he could be when he chose.

But when he'd looked at Rebecca, there had been nothing but ice. And when Dennis had tried to welcome him, Paul had treated the mayor with barely concealed contempt.

Rebecca had recovered some of her composure and was now speaking quietly to Dennis, her hand on his arm in what looked like a restraining gesture. Dennis's expression was thunderous beneath his practiced smile, but he nodded at whatever she was saying.

"I need some air," Dennis said, loud enough for those nearby to hear. "Rebecca, would you—"

"I'll stay and make sure everything's ready," Rebecca said quickly. "You go ahead."

Dennis strode toward a side door leading to the exterior

corridor, his controlled movements suggesting a man barely keeping his temper in check. Several people tracked his exit with knowing looks. Apparently, the tension between the mayor and this particular judge was not news to everyone.

Mike growled low in his throat—an unusual sound from the normally friendly schnauzer. Agatha glanced down in surprise.

"Mike, what—"

But Mike was staring at Paul Chambers, his ears still flat, his tail motionless. In all their years together, Agatha had learned to trust Mike's instincts about people. The little dog had an uncanny ability to sense when someone wasn't trustworthy. Sometimes he was wrong, of course—he'd barked at the mailman for weeks before deciding the man was acceptable—but more often than not, Mike's first impressions proved accurate. And Mike clearly did not like Paul Chambers.

Paul was now holding court with Robert Coleman, discussing something about judging criteria. His voice carried across the room—confident, knowledgeable, even charming when he laughed at something Robert said. But Agatha noticed how Marina edged away from him slightly, how her nervous energy increased when he spoke to her directly.

"Marina looks terrified of him," Emma observed quietly.

"She does, doesn't she?" Agatha sipped her cider thoughtfully. "I wonder why."

"Perhaps he is very strict as a judge?" Lorraine suggested. "Like he is strict as a health inspector?"

"Maybe." But Agatha's instincts suggested something more personal. The way Marina wouldn't meet Paul's eyes, the way she clutched her phone like a lifeline—that wasn't just professional nervousness.

Raymond Aguilar materialized beside them, his expression thoughtful. "Quite the entrance our final judge made."

"You noticed the atmosphere too?" Agatha asked.

"Hard not to. Dennis looked ready to throw a punch, and Rebecca..." Raymond shook his head. "I've never seen her look at anyone like that. Pure venom."

"What's the history?" Emma asked. "There has to be a history."

Raymond glanced around, ensuring no one was in earshot. "Twenty years ago, Paul Chambers and Rebecca were engaged."

Agatha's eyebrows rose. "Engaged?"

"Oh là là!" Lorraine clasped her hands together dramatically. "A romance gone wrong! This explains everything!"

"Rebecca broke it off," Raymond continued quietly. "Married Dennis shortly after. Paul never married. And apparently, he never forgave either of them."

"That would explain the coldness," Agatha mused. "Twenty years is a long time to hold a grudge, though."

"Some wounds run deep," Raymond said. "And from what I've heard, Paul's not the type to forgive and forget. He's made things professionally difficult for Dennis over the years—using his position as health inspector to... complicate matters."

"That seems petty," Emma said.

"Heartbreak can make people petty." Raymond's tone was philosophical. "Though I'd have thought after twenty years, everyone could at least be civil."

Agatha watched Paul Chambers laugh at something Patricia Anderson said, watched him clap Robert on the shoulder in a gesture of camaraderie. Then she looked at Rebecca, standing near the refreshment table with her rigid posture and pale face, and at Dennis returning from his cooling-off period with barely controlled fury in his eyes.

Mike whined again, pressing against Agatha's leg.

"It's all right, boy," she murmured, but she felt uneasy. The room that had seemed so festive moments ago now felt heavy with old resentments and barely concealed hostility.

At six-thirty, Dennis called for everyone's attention. His mayor's voice was back—smooth, authoritative, gracious.

"Thank you all for coming to this pre-ceremony reception," he said. "In thirty minutes, we'll proceed to the town square for the official tree lighting and judging. I want to thank our distinguished judges for traveling to Bristol Lake, and I hope you'll all find our community's Christmas spirit worthy of recognition."

Polite applause rippled through the room. Paul Chambers didn't applaud, Agatha noticed. He simply stood with his arms crossed, his expression neutral but his eyes calculating as they swept across the assembled townspeople.

As people began gathering coats and preparing to head to the square, Lorraine leaned close to Agatha.

"Mark my words, ma chérie," she whispered. "Before this night is over, there will be drama. With so much bad feeling in the air? Drama is inevitable."

Agatha wanted to disagree, wanted to believe that everyone could put aside their differences for one evening of community celebration.

But Mike's ears were still flat, his body still tense as he

watched Paul Chambers don his expensive overcoat and head toward the door without saying goodbye to anyone.

And Agatha's own instincts whispered that Lorraine might be right.

Drama was coming.

She just hoped that was all it would be.

Chapter 4

The Christmas Tree Lighting

T he town square had transformed into a winter wonderland by the time the ceremony began at seven o'clock. Agatha stood with Emma and Lorraine near the front of the crowd, Mike sitting alertly at her feet, his breath forming little clouds in the cold evening air. Around them, over two hundred people had gathered— Bristol Lake residents bundled in scarves and mittens, visitors from neighboring towns, families with children perched on shoulders to get a better view.

The magnificent Norway spruce stood dark against the twilight sky, its unlit ornaments catching the glow from the surrounding street lamps. The star sat ready at its peak, waiting for the moment of illumination.

"It's going to be beautiful," Emma breathed, her green eyes reflecting the lights from the surrounding decorations.

"Magnifique," Lorraine agreed, clutching a cup of hot cider. "Look at all the people! Bristol Lake should be very proud."

Agatha smiled, pulling her coat tighter against the cold. The square buzzed with excitement—children's laughter, the murmur of conversation, the occasional bark of a dog. Vendors had set up stations around the perimeter: Eliza's bakery stand doing brisk business in Christmas cookies, the cider station with its aromatic steam, even a small booth selling handmade ornaments with proceeds going to the food bank.

The four judges stood in a designated area near the gazebo, positioned to have the best view of the tree. Patricia Anderson held her clipboard, her severe expression softened slightly by the festive atmosphere. Robert Coleman chatted amiably with several Bristol Lake residents, his red scarf bright against his dark coat. Marina Hawkins still looked nervous, checking her phone one last time before tucking it away. And Paul Chambers stood slightly apart from the others, his expensive overcoat marking him as someone who cared about appearances, his expression neutral as he surveyed the crowd.

Dennis Crawford took his position on the gazebo steps, a microphone in hand. Rebecca stood nearby, elegant in her burgundy coat, her earlier tension masked by a gracious smile as she greeted townspeople. Whatever hostility had crackled through the community center seemed to have been set aside —at least publicly—for the ceremony.

"Good evening, everyone!" Dennis's voice boomed across the square, amplified by the speaker system. "Welcome to Bristol Lake's Annual Christmas Tree Lighting Ceremony!"

Applause and cheers erupted from the crowd. Mike's tail wagged enthusiastically.

"Tonight is special," Dennis continued, his mayor's charisma on full display. "Not only are we celebrating the Christmas season as a community, but Bristol Lake has the honor of hosting the County Christmas Tree Competition. Our distinguished judges have traveled from Rockland, Oxford Hills, Camden, and Petunia Heights to evaluate our tree, our decorations, and most importantly, our community spirit."

More applause. Agatha noticed Paul Chambers didn't join in, but his expression remained professionally neutral.

"I want to thank everyone who contributed to making this evening possible," Dennis said, and began listing committee members, volunteers, and local businesses. Eliza got a special mention for her refreshments, which made her blush and wave from her bakery stand. Raymond Aguilar was thanked for coordinating logistics. Gladys received recognition for her work with the historical society in researching traditional decorations.

The acknowledgments went on for several minutes. Agatha felt Mike shift restlessly beside her—the ceremony was lovely, but a bit long-winded for a dog's attention span.

Finally, Dennis gestured toward the tree. "And now, what we've all been waiting for. In just a moment, we'll count down together, and Bristol Lake's Christmas tree will shine for all to see. But first, let's hear from the Bristol Lake Community Choir!"

Twenty voices rose in harmony, singing "O Holy Night" with such beauty that the crowd fell silent. Agatha felt goosebumps rise on her arms that had nothing to do with the cold. Emma's eyes glistened with tears, and even Lorraine looked moved, one hand pressed to her heart.

As the choir transitioned into "Silent Night," Agatha glanced around at the crowd. Faces upturned, smiling, some singing along quietly. Children pointing at the dark tree with anticipation. Elderly couples holding hands. This was what a community was supposed to be—people coming together to celebrate something beautiful.

She noticed Paul Chambers shifting position, glancing at his watch. His expression had taken on a hint of impatience, as if the ceremony was taking longer than he'd expected. After a moment, he leaned toward Patricia Anderson and said something. She nodded without looking away from the choir.

Paul stepped back from the judge's area, moving casually toward the edge of the crowd. Agatha tracked his movement idly—he seemed to be heading around the side of the tree stand, perhaps toward the portable restrooms that had been set up behind the gazebo.

"Look, the children's choir!" Emma whispered, pulling Agatha's attention back to the gazebo where a group of elementary school students had joined the adult choir for "Jingle Bells." Their enthusiasm more than made up for their occasionally off-key notes, and the crowd erupted in delighted applause when they finished.

Mike barked happily, caught up in the festive energy.

Dennis returned to the microphone, beaming. "Thank you to our wonderful choirs! And now, the moment we've all been waiting for. When I count down from ten, we'll illuminate Bristol Lake's Christmas tree. Are you ready?"

"YES!" the crowd roared back, children's voices rising above the adults.

"All right then! Ten... nine... eight..."

The crowd joined in, voices rising together in anticipation. "Seven... six... five... four... three... two... one!"

Dennis threw the ceremonial switch.

The tree exploded into light.

Thousands of white bulbs blazed to life, transforming the Norway spruce into something magical. The gold and silver ornaments caught the light and reflected it back, creating a cascade of sparkles. The star at the top glowed brilliant white against the dark sky. The effect was breathtaking.

The crowd erupted in cheers and applause. Children squealed with delight. Someone started singing "O Christmas Tree," and others joined in. Camera flashes popped like fireflies as people captured the moment.

Agatha found herself grinning, caught up in the sheer joy of the moment. Emma grabbed her hand and squeezed it. Lorraine dabbed at her eyes with a tissue, murmuring "C'est magnifique" over and over.

Even the judges looked impressed. Patricia Anderson was making notes on her clipboard, but a small smile played at her lips. Robert Coleman clapped enthusiastically, calling out "Bravo!" Marina Hawkins had pulled out her phone to take pictures, her earlier nervousness forgotten in the beauty of the moment.

Paul Chambers was nowhere to be seen.

Agatha noticed his absence peripherally but didn't think much of it. He'd probably stepped away to use the restroom and would return in a moment. The ceremony was the important thing, and it was going beautifully.

The crowd began to mill about, some approaching the cider and cookie stations, others taking pictures with the lit tree in the background. The judges moved closer to the tree, examining the decorations, the placement of lights, the overall effect. Patricia made more notes. Robert chatted with Dennis about the ornament selection. Marina took more photos, this time of specific decoration details.

Mike tugged at his leash, wanting to explore the interesting smells near the bakery stand. Agatha held firm but gave him an extra scratch behind the ears.

"That was perfect," Emma said, her cheeks pink from cold and excitement. "Absolutely perfect. Bristol Lake has to win this year."

"The tree is certainly beautiful," Agatha agreed. "Though I suppose the judges are evaluating more than just the tree itself."

"Community spirit, civic pride, creativity, historical significance," Raymond Aguilar said, joining them with a cup of cider. "At least according to the official criteria. But really, I think it comes down to which town puts on the best show."

"Bristol Lake puts on a very good show," Lorraine declared. "The choir, the decorations, the atmosphere—parfait! And did you see Robert Coleman? He could not stop smiling. That is a good sign, non?"

The evening continued in a glow of festive warmth. Agatha chatted with various townspeople, accepted compliments on the bookstore's holiday decorations, and promised Gladys she'd attend the next book club meeting. Mike eventually settled down, content to watch the activity and accept pets from passing children.

Twenty minutes passed. Then thirty.

Agatha noticed Marina Hawkins looking around with a puzzled expression. She approached Patricia Anderson and said something. Patricia frowned and glanced at her watch, then scanned the crowd.

Robert Coleman joined them, and the three judges conferred quietly. Dennis, who'd been basking in the praise of various townspeople, noticed the huddle and made his way over.

"Is something wrong?" His voice carried slightly on the cold air.

"We're looking for Paul," Marina said. "He stepped away before the lighting, and he hasn't come back."

Dennis's expression flickered—something between relief and concern. "Perhaps he left early? Felt he'd seen enough?"

"His car is still in the parking area," Patricia said crisply. "I checked. And Paul wouldn't leave without saying goodbye. He's very professional about these things."

Robert nodded agreement. "It's not like him at all. He takes his judging responsibilities seriously."

Rebecca had joined her husband, and Agatha noticed her pale slightly at the mention of Paul's name. But her voice was steady when she spoke. "Perhaps he's still in the restroom? Or making a phone call?"

"We've checked," Marina said, her nervousness returning. "He's not at the portable toilets, he's not in the community center, and he's not answering his phone."

The festive atmosphere began to feel slightly strained as word spread through the crowd that one of the judges had gone missing. People started glancing around, as if Paul might suddenly materialize from the shadows.

Mike whined and pulled at his leash, straining toward the area behind the tree stand. Agatha absently held him back, her attention on the judges' growing concern.

"I'm sure he's fine," Dennis said with forced cheer. "Probably just stepped away to take an important call in private. You know how cell reception can be spotty around the square."

But forty-five minutes had now passed since Paul had stepped away from the judges' area. The crowd was beginning to thin as people headed home, the ceremony officially over. The tree still glowed beautifully, the decorations still sparkled, but the magic of the evening had acquired an uneasy edge.

Mike pulled harder at his leash, his attention fixed on the area behind the wooden platform that supported the tree. He whined insistently, the way he did when he wanted Agatha to pay attention to something important.

"In a minute, Mike," Agatha murmured, watching as Patricia Anderson spoke quietly but urgently with Detective Dawson, who'd been enjoying the ceremony in plain clothes. Dawson's expression shifted from relaxed to alert, and he began organizing a quiet search of the immediate area.

"Perhaps we should help look?" Emma suggested.

"I suppose it couldn't hurt," Agatha said. "Though I'm sure he'll turn up. Maybe he went to his car for something and got a phone call."

But even as she said it, she felt Mike's persistent tugging and heard his increasingly urgent whines.

"All right, boy," she said finally. "Let's take a quick look around. Then we're going home."

She had no way of knowing that in two minutes, everything would change. That the beautiful Christmas evening would become something else entirely.

That Mike's insistence was leading her toward a discovery that would shatter Bristol Lake's holiday peace.

But that realization was still two minutes away. For now, she simply followed her dog's lead, expecting nothing more dramatic than perhaps finding Paul Chambers on an important phone call, annoyed at being searched for.

She couldn't have been more wrong.

Chapter 5

Missing

Mike pulled Agatha toward the back of the tree stand with surprising determination for such a small dog. She let him lead, assuming he'd caught the scent of something interesting—probably leftover food from one of the vendors, or perhaps a cat had wandered through earlier.

"Mike, we really should head home," she said, but the schnauzer ignored her, his tail rigid with focus.

Behind them, the square was gradually emptying. Parents bundled sleepy children into cars, vendors began packing up their stations, and the remaining townspeople stood in clusters discussing the ceremony. The tree still glowed magnificently, but the festive energy had been replaced by an undercurrent of concern.

Detective Dawson had organized several volunteers to search the immediate area. Agatha could see flashlight beams bobbing through the darkness beyond the gazebo, hear voices calling Paul's name. The search was methodical but low-key —more concerned than alarmed.

"This is ridiculous," Dennis's voice carried from near the judges' area. "The man probably had an emergency and left without telling anyone. It's rude, certainly, but hardly cause for panic."

"Paul wouldn't do that," Patricia Anderson said firmly. Her clipboard was forgotten now, held loosely at her side. "Not during an official judging. He takes protocol very seriously."

"Perhaps something happened at home?" Rebecca suggested, her voice tight. "A family emergency?"

"He has no family," Marina said quietly. "Just a cousin in Portland. And she's not answering when I try to call her."

Emma appeared at Agatha's side, Lorraine trailing behind her. "Any sign of him?"

"Not yet." Agatha watched Mike sniff intently at the ground near the wooden platform that elevated the tree. "Mike seems very interested in this area, though."

"Mon Dieu, that little detective dog!" Lorraine peered into the darkness behind the platform. "What does he smell, do you think?"

"Probably a dropped cookie," Agatha said, but Mike's behavior was unusual. He wasn't excited or playful like he got when he found food. His body language was different—more intense, almost agitated.

Robert Coleman joined the small crowd near Agatha, his earlier joviality replaced by genuine worry. "This isn't like Paul at all. We've judged together for three years. He's always punctual, always professional. Even when there's been bad weather or technical problems, he never just disappears."

"How long has it been now?" Emma asked.

Patricia checked her watch. "Nearly fifty minutes since he stepped away. He left just before the tree lighting."

"I saw him head this direction," Agatha offered. "Around the side of the tree stand. I assumed he was going to the restrooms."

"We checked there," Marina said. "And the community center, and the parking area. His car is still here—I recognize it. A silver Lexus."

Dennis's expression was hard to read in the dim light, but his body language suggested impatience more than concern. "Perhaps we should just reschedule the judging evaluation for tomorrow morning. Give everyone a chance to get some rest and sort this out in daylight."

"We can't complete our evaluation without Paul," Patricia said stiffly. "The committee requires all four judges present for the final scoring."

Rebecca touched her husband's arm, a restraining gesture. "Dennis, maybe we should help with the search."

"Of course." But he didn't move, just stood watching as flashlight beams swept across the square.

Mike barked suddenly—a sharp, insistent sound that made several people jump. He was pawing at the ground now, digging at the edge of the wooden platform, his behavior growing more frantic.

"Mike, no!" Agatha moved to pull him back, embarrassed. The last thing she needed was for her dog to dig up the carefully landscaped area around the tree during an official judging. "I'm so sorry, he gets like this sometimes—"

"Wait." Raymond Aguilar had joined them, his lawyer's instincts apparently triggered by Mike's behavior. "What's he digging at?"

"I don't know. Probably caught a scent of something." Agatha tried again to pull Mike away, but the schnauzer resisted, whining urgently.

Detective Dawson approached, his flashlight beam sweeping across the ground. "Everything all right here?"

"My dog is being difficult," Agatha said apologetically. "He's fixated on this area for some reason."

Dawson knew Mike, knew about the dog's occasional role in past events—though he'd always maintained it was coincidence, not any special detecting ability. Still, he crouched down, shining his light where Mike was digging.

"Probably just an animal burrow," he said, but his tone had shifted slightly. More alert.

Mike barked again, louder this time, and lunged forward. Agatha's grip on the leash slipped, and the schnauzer scrambled toward the back edge of the platform, his paws scrabbling at the frozen ground.

"Mike!" Agatha hurried after him, acutely aware of the small crowd now watching. "I'm so sorry, he's usually much better behaved—"

She reached for Mike's collar, ready to physically drag him away if necessary. The schnauzer was pressed against the platform now, digging furiously at the base where the wooden structure met the ground.

And then Agatha saw it.

She froze, her hand hovering over Mike's collar.

Just visible beneath the edge of the platform, illuminated by the ambient glow from the Christmas tree lights, was something pale against the dark ground.

Not an animal burrow.

Not dropped food.

A hand.

Human fingers, relaxed in death, partially hidden by the wooden platform edge.

Agatha's breath caught in her throat. For a moment, she couldn't move, couldn't speak, could only stare at that pale hand lying so still against the frozen earth.

"Agatha?" Emma's voice seemed to come from very far away. "What is it? What did Mike find?"

Agatha pulled Mike back gently, her movements automatic. She heard herself speak, though her voice sounded strange to her own ears. "Detective Dawson. You need to see this."

The professional competence that came from years of reading mysteries kicked in. She didn't scream, didn't panic, simply held Mike's collar and stepped back to give Dawson room.

The detective moved forward, his flashlight beam following Agatha's line of sight. His body went rigid.

"Everyone step back," he said quietly. Then, louder: "Everyone step back now. This is a crime scene."

Emma gasped. Lorraine clutched Agatha's arm, her dramatic flair momentarily shocked into silence.

More people were gathering now, drawn by Dawson's authoritative tone. Someone asked what was wrong. A child's voice called out a question. The festive murmur of the crowd shifted into something else—confusion, concern, the beginning of fear.

Dawson had his radio out, calling for backup, for the medical examiner, for crime scene techs. His voice was steady, professional, running through protocols.

But Agatha heard the underlying tension. She understood what it meant.

Someone was dead.

And based on how long Paul Chambers had been missing, based on that too-still hand beneath the platform, based on the location and timing...

She didn't need to see the body to know who it was.

Mike pressed against her leg, whining softly. She reached down to stroke his head, her hand trembling slightly.

"Is someone hurt?" Dennis's voice, tight with something that might have been concern or might have been fear. "What's happened?"

Rebecca appeared beside him, her face pale in the Christmas lights. When she saw where Dawson was focused, where his flashlight beam illuminated that pale hand, she made a small sound—not quite a gasp, not quite a sob.

Patricia Anderson pushed forward, her professional composure cracking. "Is that—is that Paul?"

Dawson didn't answer, too focused on securing the scene, but his silence was answer enough.

The beautiful Christmas tree still glowed above them, its lights reflecting off gold and silver ornaments, its star brilliant against the dark sky. Children's laughter still echoed from the far side of the square where some families lingered, unaware of what had been discovered.

But here, in the shadow of Bristol Lake's magnificent tree, with Mike sitting quietly at Agatha's feet and the crowd beginning to whisper and speculate, Christmas had acquired a darker meaning.

Paul Chambers had come to judge a tree lighting ceremony.

He would never judge anything again.

Chapter 6

The Discovery

Within minutes, the town square transformed from a festive celebration into something else entirely. Police cruisers arrived, their lights painting the snow in alternating blue and red. Officers began stringing crime scene tape around the tree stand, their movements efficient and grim.

Agatha stood with Mike pressed against her legs, watching as Detective Dawson coordinated the response. With Sheriff Salinger away on vacation visiting his wife's family in California, Dawson had taken charge of the scene, his commands clear and efficient as officers secured the perimeter. Emma and Lorraine flanked her, both unusually quiet. Around them, the crowd had been pushed back to a safe distance, but no one seemed willing to leave. People clustered in small groups, whispering, speculating, trying to understand what had happened to their beautiful Christmas evening.

"Everyone needs to stay back," an officer called out, reinforcing the perimeter. "This is an active crime scene."

The judges stood together near the gazebo, their earlier professional demeanor shattered. Patricia Anderson's clipboard dangled forgotten from her hand, her stern face slack with shock. Robert Coleman had gone gray, one hand pressed to his chest as if steadying his heart. Marina Hawkins was crying quietly, her phone clutched uselessly in her trembling hands.

"I can't believe it," Marina whispered. "I just can't believe Paul is—"

She couldn't finish the sentence.

Dennis and Rebecca Crawford stood slightly apart from the crowd, both pale and stricken. Dennis's carefully cultivated mayor's persona had crumbled, leaving him looking older, vulnerable. Rebecca swayed slightly, and he caught her arm to steady her.

"We should go," Dennis said quietly. "There's nothing we can do here."

"We can't just leave," Rebecca's voice was barely audible. "It would look—"

"I don't care how it looks." Dennis's response was sharp. "Someone's dead. At our ceremony. We need to—" He stopped, seeming to realize people might overhear. His jaw clenched. "We need to make a statement. Later. When we know more."

Two more vehicles arrived—the medical examiner's van and a crime scene unit. Agatha watched as technicians began setting up portable lights around the tree stand, illuminating the area with harsh white brilliance that seemed obscene against the soft glow of the Christmas lights.

Detective Dawson approached her, his expression grave. "Agatha. I need to ask you some questions."

"Of course."

He pulled out a notebook, though Agatha suspected he'd remember every word regardless. "Walk me through what happened. When did you first notice something was wrong?"

Agatha took a breath, organizing her thoughts. "Mike started pulling toward this area maybe fifteen minutes ago. I thought he'd caught a scent of food or seen a cat. He was very insistent, digging at the base of the platform. I tried to stop him, and then I saw..." She gestured toward where the hand had been visible.

"You didn't touch anything?"

"No. I pulled Mike back and called you over immediately."

Dawson made a note. "Good. And before that? Did you see Paul Chambers during the ceremony?"

"Yes. He was with the other judges near the gazebo. I saw him step away just before the tree lighting—maybe five minutes before? He went around the side of the tree stand. I assumed he was heading to the restrooms."

"Did you see anyone follow him?"

Agatha thought carefully. "No. There were a lot of people around, all focused on the ceremony. I wasn't paying close attention."

"Did you notice anyone else leave the crowd around that time?"

"I don't think so. Everyone was watching the tree lighting. It was the main event."

Dawson nodded, making more notes. Emma and Lorraine stood quietly nearby, waiting their turn to be questioned.

Behind the crime scene tape, the technicians had begun

their careful work. Portable lights now fully illuminated the area behind the platform. Agatha could see officers taking photographs, measuring distances, marking evidence locations with small numbered placards.

She deliberately didn't look too closely. She'd seen enough death in her time in Bristol Lake, though not by choice. Each time, it left her shaken. Each time, she wondered how her quiet life as a bookstore owner had become entangled with such darkness.

But she also felt the familiar pull—the same instinct that drew her to mystery novels, that made her mind automatically catalog details and connections. Something about Paul's death didn't feel random. The location, the timing, during a ceremony with hundreds of witnesses...

"Agatha?" Dawson's voice pulled her back to the present. "Did you notice anything unusual about Paul's behavior at the reception earlier? Any arguments, any tension?"

Agatha hesitated. "There was tension between him and the Crawfords. Very obvious tension. Cold greetings, barely civil. And Dennis looked angry when Paul arrived."

"I noticed that too." Dawson's expression didn't change, but Agatha knew him well enough to see he was filing this information away. "Anyone else?"

"Marina Hawkins seemed nervous around him. Uncomfortable. But that might not mean anything."

"Everything might mean something right now." Dawson closed his notebook. "I'll need you to come by the station tomorrow to give a formal statement. You too, Emma, Lorraine."

"Of course," Agatha said. Lorraine nodded vigorously, and Emma murmured agreement.

One of the crime scene technicians called out to Dawson. "Detective? We're ready for you to view the body."

Dawson excused himself and ducked under the crime scene tape. Agatha watched as he approached the technician, crouching beside the body. Even from a distance, she could see his reaction—a sudden stillness, then a careful examination. When he stood, his expression was grim. He pulled out his phone and made a call, speaking too quietly for Agatha to hear.

"What do you think they found?" Emma whispered.

"Evidence," Agatha said quietly. "Something important."

Raymond Aguilar appeared beside them, his distinguished features drawn with concern. "This is terrible. Absolutely terrible. How does something like this happen in the middle of a town celebration?"

"That's what the police will try to determine," Agatha said.

"Do we know for certain it's Paul Chambers?" Raymond asked, though his tone suggested he already knew the answer.

"I think so. Based on the timing, the location, and everyone's reactions."

"Mon Dieu," Lorraine breathed. "To think, just hours ago we were all so happy, so festive. And now..."

Mike whined and pressed closer to Agatha's leg. She reached down to comfort him, her hand finding the familiar softness of his salt-and-pepper coat. Whatever he'd found, whatever instinct had driven him to dig at that spot, it had led to a grim discovery. She was grateful for his persistence, even as she wished desperately that there had been nothing to find.

Dennis Crawford was speaking urgently with Rebecca, his hand on her arm. She shook her head at something he said, her face still ashen. The other judges had been approached by officers, presumably to give statements.

The beautiful Christmas tree still glowed above the scene, its lights now seeming garish rather than magical. The star at its peak gleamed against the night sky, indifferent to the tragedy unfolding beneath it.

"Ladies and gentlemen," an officer called out to the remaining crowd. "We need everyone to clear the square. If you witnessed anything unusual this evening, please speak with an officer before you leave. Otherwise, we ask that you go home. The square will remain closed until further notice."

People began to disperse reluctantly, still whispering, still looking back toward the crime scene. Parents hurried children away, shielding them from the sight of police lights and yellow tape.

Agatha was preparing to leave when Dawson returned, his expression troubled.

"I need to speak with the Crawfords," he said, more to himself than to Agatha. But she caught the undercurrent in his voice—something more than routine questioning.

"What did you find?" she asked quietly.

Dawson hesitated, then seemed to decide she'd find out soon enough. The whole town would know by morning.

"It's Paul Chambers," he confirmed. "Stabbed. Died quickly from the wound. But the murder weapon isn't at the scene. Whoever did this either took it with them or disposed of it somewhere nearby. We'll be conducting a thorough search of the area."

Agatha's breath caught. A missing murder weapon meant the killer had been deliberate, careful. "Any other evidence?"

"We're still processing the scene. But this happened

during the ceremony, while everyone was focused on the tree lighting. Chaos of the crowd means the killer could have slipped away easily." Dawson's voice was carefully neutral. "I'll need to speak with everyone who had contact with Paul this evening, starting with the other judges and the Crawfords."

The implications hung heavy in the cold air. Behind them, the magnificent Christmas tree blazed with light, a monument to community and celebration that had become the backdrop for murder.

Mike whined again, and Agatha pulled her coat tighter against the cold.

The beautiful Christmas evening had become something else entirely.

And somewhere in Bristol Lake, a killer was walking free, perhaps confident that the missing weapon would never be found, that without it, proving murder would be nearly impossible.

Chapter 7

The Investigation Begins

Agatha arrived at the Bristol Lake Police Station at nine o'clock the next morning, Mike trotting beside her on his leash. The small brick building looked the same as always, but the atmosphere inside was charged with urgency. Officers moved purposefully between desks, phones rang constantly, and the usually quiet station buzzed with activity.

Detective Dawson looked up from his desk when she entered, his expression weary. He'd clearly been up most of the night.

"Agatha. Thank you for coming in." He gestured to the chair across from his desk. "Mike can stay if he behaves."

"He will." Agatha settled into the chair while Mike curled up at her feet. "Any developments overnight?"

Dawson rubbed his eyes, then reached for his coffee mug. "Several. The medical examiner confirmed cause of death— single stab wound to the chest. Quick, efficient. Whoever did this knew what they were doing, or got very lucky."

"Time of death?"

"Between seven-fifteen and seven-thirty last night. Right during the tree lighting ceremony, just as we suspected." Dawson pulled out a case file. "With over two hundred people in the square, all focused on the tree, the killer had perfect cover."

Agatha nodded slowly, her mind already working through the logistics. "Paul stepped away from the judges' area just before seven. I saw him go around the side of the tree stand."

"Several other witnesses confirmed that timeline. He was alive at seven-ten. Your discovery of the body was at approximately seven-fifty. So we're looking at a forty-minute window, most of which he was already dead."

"The murder weapon?" Agatha asked. "You said last night it wasn't at the scene."

Dawson's expression turned grim. "That's where things get complicated. This morning, around six-thirty, the town cleaning crew was emptying trash bins from last night's celebration. They found a knife in one of the bins near the gazebo."

He opened a folder and pulled out a photograph, sliding it across the desk. Agatha leaned forward to examine it.

The knife was beautiful in a deadly way—approximately eight inches long with an ornate silver handle decorated with intricate scrollwork. The blade gleamed even in the photograph, and the craftsmanship was clearly exceptional.

"Norwegian silver," Dawson said. "Antique, probably early 1900s. The kind of thing that gets passed down through families as an heirloom."

"You've traced it?"

"Didn't take long. I've been to enough town events at the

Crawford house to recognize their family silver collection. Dennis's grandmother emigrated from Norway in the 1920s, brought several pieces with her. This knife has been displayed in their dining room for years."

Agatha sat back, processing this information. "Dennis Crawford's knife. Found in a trash bin. After being used to murder someone he clearly disliked."

"It gets worse. Dennis's fingerprints are all over the handle. Clear, unmistakable prints."

"He used the knife at home, so of course his prints would be on it."

"Exactly what his lawyer will argue." Dawson took another sip of coffee. "But right now, we have the mayor's distinctive family heirloom used to kill a man the mayor had a very public grudge against. The knife disappeared from the Crawford house sometime before last night—we're trying to determine when it was last seen—and ended up in Paul Chambers's chest."

Agatha thought about the tension she'd witnessed at the community center reception. Dennis's barely controlled anger, Rebecca's icy demeanor toward Paul, the way both of them had seemed on edge all evening.

"Have you spoken with the Crawfords?"

"Have you spoken with the Crawfords?"

"Briefly, last night. Basic questions about their where-abouts during the ceremony, their interactions with Paul. Both seemed shocked by his death." Dawson's tone was care-fully neutral. "But now that we've found the murder weapon and traced it to their household, I need to conduct formal interviews this morning. About the knife, when it went missing, who had access to their home. Dennis's lawyer is already here, as you saw."

"Do they know yet? That it was their knife?"

"I called Dennis at seven this morning to inform him. He needs to come in to answer questions about it." Dawson's expression was grim. "He claimed he had no idea the knife was missing, said he hasn't looked at that particular display cabinet in weeks. I'll be getting the full story shortly."

"Naturally." Agatha glanced down at Mike, who was sleeping peacefully despite the serious conversation. "What about the other judges? Any of them have motive?"

"That's what I need to find out." Dawson pulled out his notebook. "Patricia Anderson seems genuinely shocked. She and Paul had judged together for years, professional relationship, no apparent conflicts. Robert Coleman the same—jovial guy, gets along with everyone, seemed to like Paul well enough."

"And Marina Hawkins?"

Dawson's expression shifted slightly. "Marina's interesting. She was visibly nervous around Paul yesterday. When I questioned her last night, she was evasive about her whereabouts during the critical timeline. Said she was 'around the square, watching the ceremony' but couldn't provide specifics."

"You think she's hiding something?"

"I think everyone's hiding something," Dawson said tiredly. "The question is whether they're hiding murder or just embarrassing secrets."

Agatha understood that all too well. Small towns were full of secrets—affairs, financial troubles, family conflicts.

Most had nothing to do with murder, but people protected them just the same.

"What about the timeline?" she asked. "Could the Crawfords have done it?"

"That's the problem. The chaos of the ceremony means almost no one can account for their exact whereabouts during those critical twenty minutes. Dennis claims he was 'circulating among the crowd, greeting constituents.' No specific alibi. Rebecca says she was 'near the gazebo, watching the ceremony.' Also no specific alibi."

"Were they together?"

"They say no. They separated during the ceremony to cover more ground, show community engagement. Very convenient for our investigation." Dawson's tone was dry.

Mike stirred at Agatha's feet, and she reached down to scratch his ears. "You're going to need help with this. Two hundred potential witnesses, multiple suspects, and a politically sensitive situation with the mayor."

"I know." Dawson met her eyes. "Which is why I'm hoping you'll be willing to ask some questions. Informally. People talk to you differently than they talk to police."

This was familiar territory now. Over the years, Agatha had found herself drawn into investigations not because she sought them out, but because circumstances—and Mike's nose for trouble—kept pulling her in. Dawson had learned to accept, if not entirely welcome, her involvement.

"Of course I'll help," Agatha said. "Though I'm not sure what I can do that you can't."

"You can talk to the book club ladies. Lorraine hears all the town gossip. Gladys knows everyone's history. Emma's plugged into the library crowd." Dawson ticked them off on his fingers. "And you have a way of getting people to open up. They don't see you as a threat."

"Just a nosy bookstore owner?"

"Just a concerned community member who happens to be very observant." Dawson's slight smile was tired but genuine. "I'll handle the formal interviews—the Crawfords, the judges, anyone with direct connection to Paul. You handle the informal intelligence gathering."

"What do we know about Paul himself? Beyond his role as a judge and health inspector?"

Dawson flipped through his notes. "Paul Chambers, forty-three, never married. County health inspector for ten years. Also volunteers as a judge for various community competitions—Christmas trees, baking contests, garden shows. Lives alone in Petunia Heights. No close family except a cousin in Portland—Loretta Thornton. We've notified her."

"Friends? Enemies?"

"That's what we need to find out. His professional life as a health inspector means he made decisions that affected people's livelihoods. Restaurant violations, closures, citations. Could be relevant."

"Or it could be entirely personal. That tension between Paul and the Crawfords was twenty years old."

"Twenty years is a long time to hold a grudge," Dawson said, echoing Agatha's thought from the previous evening. "But murder suggests someone reached a breaking point."

The station door opened, and an officer escorted Dennis Crawford inside, followed by a man in an expensive suit who was clearly his attorney. Dennis looked haggard, his usual polish dimmed by lack of sleep and stress. When he saw

Agatha, something flickered across his face—surprise, perhaps, or wariness.

"I need to take this interview," Dawson said quietly. "Can you start by talking to the other judges? Get their impressions of Paul, any observations from last night?"

"Where are they?"

"Patricia and Robert are staying at the Harborside Inn. Marina's staying with a friend in town—I'll text you the address." He stood, gathering his files. "Be careful, Agatha. Whoever did this was comfortable enough to commit murder in the middle of a crowded celebration. That suggests either desperation or dangerous confidence."

"I'll be careful." Agatha rose, Mike instantly alert at her feet. "And Dawson? The knife being found in the trash—that suggests panic. Someone trying to dispose of evidence quickly."

"I thought the same thing. Killer commits the murder, panics when they realize how distinctive and traceable the weapon is, tosses it in the nearest trash bin." Dawson's expression was grim. "Unfortunately for Dennis Crawford, that knife leads straight back to him."

"You think he did it?"

"Right now? He's my primary suspect. His knife, his motive, his opportunity, no alibi." Dawson ticked off the points. "When evidence points this clearly in one direction, I have to follow it."

"Even though he's the mayor?"

"Especially because he's the mayor. I can't give him special treatment just because of his position." Dawson glanced toward the interview room where Dennis waited. "If he killed Paul Chambers, he'll answer for it like anyone else."

Agatha nodded slowly, though something nagged at her. The evidence seemed almost too perfect, too obvious. But maybe that was just her love of mystery novels talking—sometimes the obvious answer really was the right one.

As Agatha walked down Central Avenue toward the Harborside Inn, Mike trotting contentedly beside her, she felt the familiar pull of a mystery that needed solving. Paul Chambers had died during what should have been a joyful community celebration, and the ripples of his death were spreading through Bristol Lake like cracks in ice.

Someone in this town knew what had happened behind that Christmas tree stand.

And Agatha intended to find out who.

Chapter 8

Suspects and Motives

By late afternoon, word had spread through Bristol Lake like wildfire. Agatha had barely unlocked the door to One Deadly Chapter when Emma hurried in, followed closely by Lorraine and Gladys. All three looked shaken, their usual cheerfulness replaced by somber concern.

"Emergency book club meeting," Emma announced, though it was hardly necessary. Mike greeted each of them with his usual enthusiasm, tail wagging, providing a small moment of normalcy in an otherwise grim day.

"The whole town is talking about nothing else," Gladys said, settling into one of the café chairs with a heavy sigh. "I've lived in Bristol Lake for eighty years, and I can count on one hand the number of murders we've had. And never during a Christmas celebration."

"C'est terrible," Lorraine added, unwinding her purple scarf with less than her usual dramatic flair. "To think, we were all there, all so happy, and someone was committing murder just steps away from us."

Agatha locked the front door and flipped the sign to

"Closed." The bookstore felt like the right place for this conversation—private, comfortable, and far from prying ears. She made a pot of coffee while the others gathered around the café table, Mike settling beneath it with a contented sigh.

"What have you heard?" Emma asked as Agatha brought mugs to the table. "We know you went to the police station this morning. What did Detective Dawson say?"

Agatha measured her words carefully. "Paul was stabbed. Single wound, quick. The murder weapon was found this morning in a trash bin—a distinctive Norwegian silver knife that belongs to the Crawfords."

The reaction was immediate. Lorraine gasped dramatically, Gladys's eyes widened, and Emma's hand flew to her mouth.

"Dennis Crawford's knife?" Gladys said. "You're certain?"

"Dawson confirmed it. Family heirloom from Dennis's grandmother. His fingerprints are on it, which makes sense since it's his own knife from his house."

"Mon Dieu," Lorraine breathed. "This looks very bad for the mayor, non?"

"It looks terrible for him," Agatha admitted. "He had motive—everyone saw the tension between him and Paul last night. He had means—it was his own knife. And he has no real alibi for the time of the murder."

"But surely Dennis wouldn't be so stupid," Emma said. "If you were going to kill someone, would you use your own distinctive family knife and then throw it in a trash bin where anyone could find it?"

"People panic," Gladys said thoughtfully. "Even intelligent people make foolish decisions in the moment. Though I agree, it does seem rather obvious."

Agatha pulled out a notebook—not to play detective, exactly, but because organizing information was second nature to her. Years of cataloging books and solving puzzles in mystery novels had given her a systematic mind.

"What do we actually know about Paul Chambers?" she asked. "Beyond the basics?"

"He was the county health inspector," Emma said. "And he judged various community competitions. My colleague at the library said he was very strict—some people thought too strict."

"Strict is one word for it," Gladys said, her tone sharp. "I remember when he shut down that little Italian restaurant in Petunia Heights two years ago. The family was devastated. They claimed the violations were exaggerated, but Paul was adamant."

"Was that Villa Toscana Restaurant?" Agatha asked, remembering Dawson mentioning Paul's professional role might have made him enemies.

"I believe so, yes. Such a shame. The food was wonderful." Gladys shook her head. "But Paul took his responsibilities very seriously. Perhaps too seriously."

Lorraine leaned forward conspiratorially. "But there is more to the story with Dennis and Rebecca, mes amies. Much more."

"We know there was tension," Agatha said. "Everyone saw it last night."

"Ah, but do you know why?" Lorraine's eyes gleamed with the thrill of sharing choice gossip. "Twenty years ago, Paul Chambers and Rebecca were engaged to be married."

Emma's eyes widened. "What?"

"Oui! They were planning a wedding, had set a date, everything. And then..." Lorraine paused dramatically, "Rebecca broke off the engagement. She discovered Paul had been dishonest about something—I do not know what, exactly. But she ended things and married Dennis instead."

"And Paul never forgave her," Gladys added. "Or Dennis. There's been bad blood between them ever since. Professional jealousy, personal resentment. Paul seemed to take every opportunity to make things difficult for Dennis politically."

Agatha made notes, her mind working through the implications. "So Dennis had a twenty-year grudge against Paul. And Rebecca had her own complicated history with him."

"It gives them both motive," Emma said quietly. "Though I can't imagine Rebecca committing murder. She seems so... composed. Elegant."

"Elegant people can be desperate people," Gladys observed. "And desperate people do terrible things."

Mike stirred under the table, and Agatha reached down to scratch his ears. The little schnauzer had been the one to find Paul's body, following some instinct that had led him straight to the evidence. She wished he could tell her what else he'd sensed last night—who'd been where, what he'd smelled, whether anyone had acted suspiciously.

"What about the other judges?" Emma asked. "Could one of them have had a reason to kill Paul?"

"Patricia Anderson seems very professional," Agatha said. "She and Paul had judged together for years. Dawson said there's no apparent conflict."

"And Robert Coleman is such a cheerful man," Lorraine

added. "He loves his cookies and his Christmas celebrations. I cannot imagine him murdering anyone."

"That leaves Marina Hawkins," Gladys said. "The nervous one who kept checking her phone. Did you notice how uncomfortable she seemed around Paul?"

Agatha had noticed. "Dawson said she was evasive when he questioned her. Couldn't provide a specific alibi for the time of the murder."

"Professional jealousy, perhaps?" Emma suggested. "Maybe Paul blocked her from some judging position, or criticized her work?"

"It's possible." Agatha made another note. "Though murder seems extreme for professional rivalry."

They sat in silence for a moment, the warmth of the bookstore café a sharp contrast to the dark subject of their conversation. Outside, Central Avenue was quieter than usual—people hurrying home rather than lingering to chat, the Christmas decorations that had seemed so festive yesterday now carrying a more somber weight.

"The thing is," Agatha said slowly, "the evidence points very clearly to Dennis. His knife, his motive, his opportunity. It's almost too clear."

"You think someone is framing him?" Lorraine's dramatic instincts perked up. "Like in an Agatha Christie novel!"

"I don't know what I think yet. But something feels..." Agatha struggled for the right word. "Convenient. If you wanted to frame someone for murder, using their own distinctive knife would be a good way to do it."

"But who would want to frame Dennis?" Emma asked. "And why?"

"Those are good questions," Gladys said. "Though I can

think of several people in town who aren't particularly fond of our mayor. He can be rather condescending."

"Not liking someone isn't the same as framing them for murder," Agatha pointed out. "You'd need serious motive for that level of malice."

"Or you'd need to be covering your own crime," Gladys said shrewdly. "Kill Paul, use Dennis's knife, let Dennis take the fall. Two birds with one stone."

It was an unsettling thought. Agatha looked at her notes —a list of suspects, motives, questions without answers. This was the part she'd always loved about mystery novels: piecing together clues, considering possibilities, watching patterns emerge. But in real life, there was no guarantee of a neat solution, no assurance that justice would prevail.

"So what do we do?" Emma asked, looking at Agatha expectantly.

"We ask questions," Agatha said. "Quietly, carefully. We talk to people, we listen to what they say and what they don't say. We see if anything doesn't fit."

"Like we have before," Lorraine said with satisfaction.

"But carefully," Agatha emphasized. "Someone committed murder last night in the middle of a crowded celebration. They're either very desperate or very confident. Either way, they're dangerous."

Gladys nodded approvingly. "The voice of reason. I approve. So where do we start?"

"I'm going to talk to the judges," Agatha said. "Get their impressions of Paul, find out if there were any conflicts we don't know about. Emma, can you check at the library? See if anyone remembers Paul from past events, any incidents or problems?"

"Of course." Emma pulled out her own notebook. "The library is gossip central. Someone will know something."

"And I," Lorraine declared, "will talk to everyone I know. Which is everyone in Bristol Lake. If there are secrets about Paul Chambers, I will uncover them!"

"Discreetly," Agatha reminded her.

"But of course, ma chérie! I am the soul of discretion."

Emma and Agatha exchanged glances but didn't contradict her. Lorraine's version of discretion might not be subtle, but she did have an uncanny ability to extract information from people.

"What about the Crawfords?" Gladys asked. "Are we assuming they're innocent, or are they on our suspect list?"

"Everyone's on the list until we know more," Agatha said. "Though I have a hard time believing Dennis would be foolish enough to use his own knife and then dispose of it so carelessly."

"Unless he panicked," Emma said. "Like you mentioned earlier."

"Maybe." But Agatha's instincts said there was more to this story. The knife, the timing, the very public nature of the crime—something didn't quite fit together yet.

Mike stretched beneath the table, yawning widely. He seemed unconcerned by talk of murder and suspects, content in the warmth of the bookstore with his favorite people nearby.

"It's settled then," Gladys said, rising from her chair. "We investigate. Carefully, quietly, and above all, safely. No confronting potential killers alone."

"Agreed," Agatha said firmly. "And we share everything

we learn. No holding back information because it seems unimportant. Small details matter."

They gathered their coats and scarves, preparing to venture back out into the cold December evening. The Christmas tree in the town square would still be lit, Agatha knew, though she doubted many people would stop to admire it tonight. The celebration had been tainted, the joy dimmed by violence and death.

As her friends filed out, Emma lingered at the door. "Do you really think Dennis might be innocent?"

"I think the evidence against him is convenient," Agatha said carefully. "Maybe too convenient. But I could be wrong. Maybe sometimes the obvious answer really is the right one."

"But you don't think so."

"I think we need to find out more before jumping to conclusions." Agatha locked the door behind Emma and looked down at Mike, who'd come to stand beside her. "What do you think, boy? Who killed Paul Chambers?"

Mike wagged his tail, completely unhelpful.

Agatha smiled despite everything and prepared to head home to 93 Knob Hill. Tomorrow she'd start asking questions, following leads, trying to piece together what had happened during those crucial minutes behind the Christmas tree.

But tonight, she'd do what she always did when faced with a puzzle: she'd make tea, curl up with Mike beside her, and think.

Because somewhere in what she'd seen and heard last night, there had to be a clue. Something that would point toward the truth.

Chapter 9

The Judges

The Harborside Inn sat at the edge of Bristol Lake's small harbor, a charming Victorian building with a wraparound porch and views of the water. Agatha had called ahead, and the innkeeper had confirmed that Patricia Anderson and Robert Coleman were both still in residence, though their original plan had been to leave this morning.

"Murder does complicate travel plans," the innkeeper had said dryly over the phone.

Now Agatha stood in the inn's cozy sitting room, Mike at her feet, waiting while the innkeeper went to fetch the judges. The room was decorated for Christmas—a small tree in the corner, garlands over the fireplace, the scent of cinnamon and cloves from a simmering pot in the kitchen. It should have felt festive. Instead, it felt sad, like a party abandoned mid-celebration.

Patricia Anderson appeared first, her severe black coat replaced by a charcoal cardigan, but her stern expression unchanged. Her gray hair was pulled back in a tight bun, and she carried her ever-present clipboard, though it hung loosely at her side.

"Miss Royale," she said, her tone professional but not unfriendly. "The innkeeper said you wanted to speak with me about the night of the incident."

"If you have a few minutes," Agatha said. "I know Detective Dawson has already questioned you, but I'm trying to piece together what happened. For the community's sake."

Patricia's expression softened slightly. "I understand. Please, sit."

They settled into armchairs near the fireplace. Mike curled up at Agatha's feet, his presence seeming to relax Patricia marginally. Even stern judges, apparently, were not immune to a friendly schnauzer's charm.

"Paul's death is a terrible shock," Patricia began without preamble. "We've judged together for nearly five years. He was professional, knowledgeable, took his responsibilities seriously. Perhaps too seriously, at times."

"Too seriously?" Agatha prompted gently.

"Paul believed in absolute standards. No exceptions, no leniency. Whether judging a Christmas tree or conducting a health inspection, he held everyone to the strictest criteria." Patricia's lips pursed. "It made him effective, but not always popular."

"Did that create conflicts?"

"Occasionally. Last year, he gave a very low score to a town that many felt deserved better. There were complaints to the competition committee, accusations of bias. But Paul stood by his evaluation, and the committee supported him."

"What about his personal life? Did you know him well outside of judging?"

Patricia shook her head. "We were colleagues, not friends. He was a private person. Never spoke much about his life in Petunia Heights, his work as a health inspector, anything personal. Our conversations were limited to the competitions we judged."

"What about last night? When did you last see him?"

"Just before the tree lighting. He mentioned stepping away briefly—I assumed to use the restroom or make a phone call. He seemed... tense. More than usual."

"Tense how?"

"Distracted. He kept looking toward where the Crawfords were standing. I noticed the obvious tension between them at the reception, of course. Everyone did." Patricia's expression was disapproving. "Very unprofessional, allowing personal conflicts to intrude on official duties."

"Where were you during the ceremony?" Agatha asked, keeping her tone conversational rather than interrogative.

"I was watching the tree lighting initially, making notes for my evaluation. Then nature called—too much coffee at the reception." A slight smile ghosted across her stern features. "I went to the portable restrooms behind the community center. There was quite a line. I was in there for at least fifteen minutes, perhaps longer."

"Can anyone confirm that?"

"Several women from Oxford Hills. We commiserated about the cold and the wait. One of them made a joke about poor planning for facilities at a large event." Patricia's tone suggested she'd agreed with the assessment. "Detective Dawson has their names. I'm sure he's verified my statement."

Agatha nodded. A fifteen-minute wait in a bathroom line

with witnesses meant Patricia had a solid alibi for the critical timeline.

"Do you have any thoughts on who might have wanted to harm Paul?"

Patricia was quiet for a moment, considering. "Paul made decisions that affected people's livelihoods. Harsh inspection reports, low competition scores, strict adherence to rules. I'm sure he had enemies, though I couldn't name them specifically. But murder?" She shook her head. "That seems extreme."

"Unless the motive was personal rather than professional," Agatha suggested.

"You're thinking of the Crawfords." It wasn't a question. "Yes, that tension was impossible to miss. But I can't believe a sitting mayor would commit murder over a twenty-year-old grudge. Can you?"

It was a fair question. Agatha thanked Patricia for her time and went to find Robert Coleman, who was apparently in the dining room enjoying a late breakfast.

She found him at a corner table, working his way through what appeared to be pancakes, bacon, and enough coffee to fuel a small village. His cheerful red scarf hung on the back of his chair, and his round face brightened when he saw Agatha approach.

"Ah! The bookstore detective!" He gestured to an empty chair. "Please, join me. Have you eaten? The pancakes here are exceptional."

"I'm fine, thank you." Agatha sat, Mike settling beside her chair. "I was hoping to ask you a few questions about last night."

"Of course, of course." Robert's jovial expression dimmed. "Terrible business. Just terrible. Poor Paul."

"How well did you know him?"

"We judged together for three years, various competitions around the county. Christmas trees, baking contests, garden shows. Paul was very knowledgeable, very thorough in his evaluations." Robert took a bite of pancake, chewing thoughtfully. "To be honest, he beat me out for the head judge position last year. I was disappointed, naturally, but he was the better choice. More experienced, more respected by the committee."

"Were you upset about that?" Agatha asked carefully.

"Upset? Oh, for about a day, perhaps." Robert laughed, a genuine sound. "But I enjoy judging regardless of the title. And Paul earned the position fairly. No hard feelings."

His easy admission and obvious lack of resentment rang true. Agatha found it hard to imagine this cheerful man harboring murderous intent over a judging position.

"What about last night? When did you last see Paul?"

"Just before the tree lighting. He seemed preoccupied, stepped away from our group. I thought he might be getting a better angle to view the tree, or perhaps taking photographs. Some judges are very particular about documentation." Robert sipped his coffee. "I went to get some cookies from that wonderful bakery—what's it called?"

"Eliza's Cottage Bakery & Patisserie."

"That's it! Marvelous scones, exceptional Christmas cookies. I bought a dozen to take back to my wife." He pulled a receipt from his pocket, smoothing it on the table. "See? Timestamp is seven-eighteen. I was there for at least ten minutes, chatting with the baker—delightful woman—and several other customers. By the time I returned to the judging area, everyone was looking for Paul."

Agatha noted the receipt details. Another solid alibi. Robert had been at Eliza's bakery, surrounded by witnesses, during the critical timeline.

"Did you notice any tension between Paul and anyone else? Besides the obvious issue with the Crawfords?"

"Marina seemed uncomfortable around him," Robert said, lowering his voice. "She and Paul had worked together on various judging panels, but lately there's been... tension. I don't know the details, but I sensed friction."

"What kind of friction?"

"Professional, I assumed. Paul was very strict about ethics, protocol, proper procedures. If he thought another judge wasn't following guidelines..." Robert shrugged. "He could be quite critical."

This aligned with what Agatha had observed—Marina's nervousness, her constant phone-checking, the way she'd avoided Paul's direct gaze.

"One more question," Agatha said. "You mentioned Paul was very thorough in his evaluations. What did you mean by that?"

"Paul believed in complete assessments. He didn't just look at the obvious—the appearance of a Christmas tree, for example. He researched the town's history, the committee's budget, the community involvement. He was thorough in everything he did, whether judging competitions or conducting health inspections." Robert's expression turned thoughtful. "Sometimes that thoroughness uncovered things people preferred to keep hidden."

"What kind of things?"

"Oh, I don't know specifics. Just an impression that Paul's investigations—whether official or unofficial—sometimes revealed uncomfortable truths. He wasn't one to overlook irregularities."

Agatha filed this information away. Paul's thoroughness, his strict adherence to rules, his tendency to uncover secrets —all of these could make enemies.

She thanked Robert and asked the innkeeper where she might find Marina Hawkins. The woman was staying with a friend on Maple Street, just a few blocks away.

The house was a modest Cape Cod with blue shutters and a small front porch. Marina answered the door herself, her highlighted hair less perfectly styled than yesterday, her expression immediately wary when she saw Agatha.

"Miss Royale? Is something wrong?"

"I was hoping to ask you a few questions about last night. Just trying to understand what happened."

Marina hesitated, then stepped outside onto the porch, pulling the door closed behind her. "My friend is resting. We can talk out here."

She didn't offer to sit, didn't suggest they go somewhere warmer. Her body language screamed discomfort, and she kept glancing toward the street as if worried someone might see them talking.

"I've already spoken with Detective Dawson," Marina said. "I told him everything I know."

"I understand. But sometimes talking through events helps clarify things. Can you tell me about Paul? How well did you know him?"

"We judged together. Professional relationship, nothing more."

"Patricia and Robert both mentioned that Paul was very thorough. Very strict about following rules and protocols."

Marina's face paled slightly. "Yes. He was... very particular about proper procedures."

"Did that create any conflicts between you?"

"I don't know what you mean." But her hand went to her phone in her pocket, a nervous gesture.

"Marina, Paul is dead. If there was something—anything—that might help explain what happened, now is the time to share it."

"I don't know anything about his death." Marina's voice rose slightly. "I was at the ceremony, watching the tree lighting like everyone else."

"Where exactly were you?"

"In the crowd. Near the back of the square."

"Can anyone confirm that? Did you stand with anyone, talk to anyone during those minutes?"

Marina's nervous energy increased. "There were hundreds of people there. I was just... around. Watching the ceremony."

"You can't provide any specific details about your whereabouts?"

"I already told Detective Dawson this. I was there, at the ceremony. That's all I can tell you." Marina wrapped her arms around herself, shivering in the cold. "I'm sorry about Paul. Truly. But I don't know anything that could help your investigation."

"This isn't my investigation," Agatha said gently. "I'm just trying to understand what happened to someone in our community."

"Then talk to the Crawfords." Marina's response was

sharp, almost bitter. "Everyone knows they hated Paul. Everyone saw how they treated him last night. If you're looking for someone with a motive, start there."

With that, she turned and went back inside, closing the door with more force than necessary.

Agatha stood on the porch for a moment, Mike pressing against her leg. Marina was hiding something, that much was clear. Whether it was relevant to Paul's murder or simply a personal secret she wanted to protect remained to be seen.

But her nervousness, her evasive answers, her inability— or unwillingness—to provide a solid alibi... all of it raised questions.

Agatha pulled out her notebook and made notes as she walked back toward Central Avenue. Patricia Anderson: solid alibi, no apparent motive. Robert Coleman: solid alibi, seemed genuinely fond of Paul despite professional competition. Marina Hawkins: no alibi, obviously hiding something, uncomfortable discussing Paul's "thoroughness."

The judges were clearing themselves one by one. Or at least, two of them were.

Marina remained a question mark—nervous, evasive, and increasingly suspicious.

But was she nervous because she'd committed murder? Or because Paul had discovered some secret she desperately wanted to keep hidden?

Chapter 10

The Crawfords' Silence

Agatha spotted Dennis Crawford through the window of Bristol Lake Town Hall as she passed by on her morning walk with Mike. The mayor sat at a conference table visible from the street, papers spread before him, his posture rigid with tension. A man in an expensive suit sat beside him—his lawyer, Agatha assumed.

On impulse, she pushed open the door and stepped inside. The receptionist looked up in surprise.

"Miss Royale! Can I help you?"

"I was hoping to speak with Mayor Crawford for just a moment. If he's available."

The receptionist glanced toward the conference room uncertainly. "He's with his attorney. I don't think—"

"It's fine, Diane." Dennis's voice carried from the open doorway. He stood, his expression unreadable. "Miss Royale can spare a few minutes."

Agatha left Mike with the receptionist, who seemed happy for the distraction, and entered the conference room.

The lawyer—she recognized him now as Marcus Thornhill, one of the county's top defense attorneys—watched her with sharp, assessing eyes.

"Mr. Crawford," Agatha began. "I wanted to—"

"If you're here to ask questions on behalf of the police," Thornhill interrupted smoothly, "my client has already been interviewed by Detective Dawson."

"I'm not with the police. I'm just... the bookstore owner who found the body. I'm trying to understand what happened."

Dennis gestured to a chair, though his movements were stiff. Up close, he looked worse than she'd expected—pale, with dark circles under his eyes, his usually impeccable appearance slightly disheveled.

"What do you want to know?" His voice was flat, exhausted.

Agatha sat carefully. "The knife that was found. It belonged to you?"

"You already know it did. The whole town knows by now." Dennis's hands clenched on the table. "It's from my grandmother's collection. Family heirloom. And yes, before you ask, my fingerprints are on it because it's my knife. I've handled it dozens of times over the years."

"When did you last see it?"

"I don't know. Weeks? I don't pay attention to the display cabinet." His frustration was evident. "Rebecca would be more likely to notice household details."

"Can you tell me about your relationship with Paul Chambers?"

Dennis's jaw tightened. "Old history. Personal matters that have nothing to do with his death."

"But surely—"

"My client doesn't have to explain his personal feelings," Thornhill cut in. "Disliking someone isn't evidence of murder."

Agatha tried a different approach. "Where were you during the tree lighting? When Paul was killed?"

"I was there. At the ceremony. Doing my job as mayor." Dennis's response sounded rehearsed, as if he'd said it multiple times already. "Greeting constituents, making sure the event ran smoothly."

"Can anyone verify—"

"There were two hundred people there, Miss Royale. I spoke with dozens of them. I can't give you a minute-by-minute accounting of every conversation." His control was slipping, voice rising slightly. "I was working, being visible, being accessible. I wasn't keeping track because I had no reason to think someone was being murdered with my own knife."

"Mr. Crawford, if you didn't kill Paul, then someone is framing you. Someone who had access to your house, who knew about the tension between you and Paul—"

"I know that." Dennis stood abruptly, turning away from her. "Don't you think I know that? Someone was in my home, took my grandmother's knife, used it to commit murder, and now everyone in Bristol Lake thinks I'm a killer."

"Then help me find out who really did it."

Dennis turned back to face her, and for a moment she saw past the mayor's facade to the terrified man beneath. "How? I don't know who took the knife. I don't know when. I don't know anything except that my life is being destroyed and I can't stop it."

"Dennis," Thornhill said quietly, a warning in his tone.

"What about Rebecca?" Agatha asked. "Could she—"

"Leave my wife out of this." Dennis's response was sharp, immediate. "Rebecca had nothing to do with any of this. Nothing."

"But—"

"This conversation is over," Thornhill said, standing. "Miss Royale, I appreciate your concern, but my client has said all he's going to say. If you want more information, speak with Detective Dawson."

Agatha recognized a dismissal when she heard one. She stood, thanked them for their time, and left the conference room. As she collected Mike from the receptionist, she heard Dennis's voice through the still-open door.

"This is hopeless, Marcus. The evidence, the motive, everything points to me. Even she thinks I did it."

"We'll fight this," Thornhill replied. "But you need to tell me everything, Dennis. No more holding back."

Agatha didn't hear Dennis's response as she pushed open the door and stepped into the cold December morning.

TWENTY MINUTES LATER, she sat across from Detective Dawson at the police station, Mike at her feet. Dawson did not look pleased.

"You questioned Dennis Crawford?" His tone was carefully controlled. "Agatha, he's the primary suspect in a murder investigation. You can't just walk up and interrogate him."

"I didn't interrogate. I asked a few questions."

"Questions that could compromise the investigation if his lawyer decides you were acting as an agent of the police."

"I wasn't—"

"I know you weren't. But Thornhill could argue you were. It's a problem." Dawson rubbed his eyes tiredly. "What did Dennis tell you?"

"That he doesn't know when the knife went missing, that his prints are on it because it's his knife, that he can't provide a specific alibi because he was 'doing his job as mayor.'" Agatha paused. "And he got very defensive when I mentioned Rebecca. Said she had nothing to do with it and to leave her out of it."

"Same as what he told me in his official interview this morning." Dawson made a note. "He's hiding something. Whether it's guilt over murder or something else, I can't tell yet."

"He looked terrified."

"Guilty people often do when they realize they're caught." But Dawson's tone suggested he wasn't entirely convinced either. "I'm interviewing Rebecca this afternoon. Maybe she'll be more forthcoming."

"Did you get anything else from Dennis? Anything that might point to someone else?"

Dawson hesitated, then seemed to decide sharing information was acceptable. "He confirmed multiple people have had access to his house—cleaning service, various town committees, social events. The knife could have been taken anytime in the past few weeks and he wouldn't have noticed."

"So dozens of potential suspects."

"Or the obvious suspect right in front of us." Dawson closed his file. "Agatha, I appreciate your help. I do. But please don't approach Dennis or Rebecca again without clearing it with me first. This is a sensitive situation, and I can't have civilians muddying the waters."

"Of course. I'm sorry."

"Don't be sorry. Just be careful." His expression softened slightly. "And if you learn anything useful, you know where to find me."

"What about Rebecca? Are you going to question her?"

"This afternoon. I've asked her to come in." Dawson glanced at his watch. "She's due here in about an hour. Maybe she'll be more forthcoming than her husband."

"Dennis was very protective of her when I mentioned her name."

"I noticed that in his interview too. Either he's trying to shield her from suspicion, or he knows she's involved somehow." Dawson tapped his pen against his desk. "Or he's just being a protective husband. Hard to say."

Agatha was about to respond when Dawson's phone rang. He answered, listened for a moment, then his expression changed—surprise mixed with concern.

"When? ... I see. ... No, don't let her leave. I'll be right there."

He hung up and looked at Agatha. "That was Officer Martinez. He's at the Harborside Inn. Apparently Marina Hawkins just tried to check out and leave town. When he informed her she couldn't leave without clearing it with me first, she became extremely agitated."

"Agitated how?"

"She said, and I quote, 'You don't understand. Paul was

going to ruin everything. You have no idea what he was capable of.'" Dawson grabbed his coat. "I need to bring her in for questioning. Now."

He hurried out, leaving Agatha sitting in the station with Mike. She sat there for a moment, processing what she'd just heard.

Paul was going to ruin everything.

Marina's nervous behavior suddenly made terrible sense —not the nervousness of someone uncomfortable around a strict colleague, but the panic of someone whose secrets were about to be exposed.

What had Marina been hiding? What had Paul's thoroughness uncovered that she was so desperate to protect?

Agatha stood slowly, Mike immediately alert at her feet. Two suspects, both with secrets they were desperately trying to hide. Dennis Crawford, who wouldn't explain his hatred of Paul and couldn't account for his whereabouts during the murder. Marina Hawkins, who was hiding something Paul had discovered and was now trying to flee town.

But something still felt wrong about both of them.

The knife. It always came back to the knife.

Someone had taken that Norwegian silver blade from the Crawford house. Someone had used it to kill Paul Chambers. Someone had thrown it in a trash bin, either in panic or in a calculated attempt to frame Dennis.

Agatha walked slowly toward the door, her mind working through the puzzle. Dennis had access to his own knife, certainly, but would he be foolish enough to use such a distinctive family heirloom? Marina seemed panicked and desperate, but when would she have had access to the Crawford house to steal the knife?

Neither scenario quite fit.

She stepped outside into the cold December air, Mike trotting beside her as they headed back toward Central Avenue. The Christmas decorations that lined the street seemed garish now in the daylight, a reminder of the celebration that had turned deadly.

People passed her on the sidewalk, some offering greetings, others averting their eyes—everyone in Bristol Lake knew she'd found the body, knew she was somehow involved in yet another investigation. Some probably thought she attracted trouble. Maybe they were right.

But as Agatha walked past the town square where the Christmas tree still stood—beautiful and terrible, a monument to community and murder—she couldn't shake the feeling that she was missing something crucial.

Something everyone had seen but no one had properly understood.

Marina's panic. Dennis's terror. Rebecca's evasiveness. The knife in the trash bin. Paul's corruption and thoroughness and twenty-year-old grudges.

All the pieces were there, scattered like ornaments after a tree had fallen.

She just had to figure out how they fit together.

Mike whined softly and pressed against her leg, and Agatha looked down at her loyal companion. "What do you think, boy? What are we missing?"

Mike tilted his head, his dark eyes unreadable, and Agatha couldn't help but smile despite everything.

Somewhere in Bristol Lake, a killer was walking free, perhaps confident that Dennis Crawford would take the fall.

Perhaps relieved that Marina's panic was drawing attention away from them.

But Agatha had learned over the years that killers made mistakes. They always did, eventually.

And when this one did, she intended to be there to catch it.

Chapter 11

Rebecca's Secret

Agatha had debated all morning whether approaching Rebecca Crawford was wise. The woman's husband was the prime suspect in a murder investigation, and Agatha had no official standing to ask questions. But something about the way Dennis had protected Rebecca during his police interview, the way he'd insisted she had nothing to do with Paul's death—it nagged at her.

So when she saw Rebecca's car pull up outside the Bristol Lake Community Center late that afternoon, Agatha made a decision. She crossed the street with Mike trotting beside her, catching Rebecca just as she was locking her vehicle.

"Rebecca? Do you have a moment?"

Rebecca turned, and Agatha was struck by how different she looked from the composed woman at the tree lighting ceremony. Her elegant coat hung loosely on her frame as if she'd lost weight overnight, and her carefully styled hair was pulled back in a simple ponytail. Dark circles shadowed her eyes.

"Miss Royale." Rebecca's voice was brittle, carefully controlled. "If you're here on behalf of the police—"

"I'm not," Agatha said quickly. "I'm just... I'm trying to understand what happened. As someone who was there, who saw Paul die."

Rebecca flinched at the name. Her hand tightened on her car keys. "I don't know what I can tell you that I haven't already told Detective Dawson."

"Maybe we could just talk? Woman to woman, not officially. Just..." Agatha gestured helplessly. "This has affected the whole town. All of us are trying to make sense of it."

For a moment, Rebecca looked as though she might refuse. Then something in her expression crumbled slightly. "All right. But not here. Too many people."

They walked to a small park two blocks away, deserted in the December cold except for a few hardy birds pecking at the frozen ground. Rebecca sat on a bench, and Agatha settled beside her, Mike lying at their feet.

For a long moment, neither spoke. Then Rebecca said quietly, "Everyone thinks Dennis killed him."

"The evidence looks bad," Agatha admitted. "But evidence isn't always what it seems."

"The knife was his. Everyone knows that now." Rebecca's voice was hollow. "Our family heirloom, used to kill a man we both hated. How convenient."

"Did you hate him?"

Rebecca turned to look at Agatha directly for the first time. "You want the truth? Yes. I hated Paul Chambers. I hated him for twenty years."

The raw honesty in her voice was startling. Agatha waited, sensing there was more.

"I suppose everyone knows by now," Rebecca continued. "We weren't exactly subtle at the reception. Paul and I were engaged once. A lifetime ago, it feels like now."

"What happened?"

"He cheated on me." Rebecca's laugh was bitter. "Such a cliché, isn't it? But it wasn't just the affair. It was discovering that he was dishonest about so many things. His work, his finances, his character. The man I thought I was going to marry didn't exist. He was a carefully constructed facade hiding someone manipulative and cruel."

Agatha could hear the old pain in Rebecca's voice, still raw after all these years.

"I broke off the engagement. Met Dennis shortly after—he was everything Paul wasn't. Honest, straightforward, genuinely kind. We married within a year, and I never looked back." Rebecca pulled her coat tighter. "Or I thought I hadn't looked back. But seeing Paul at the ceremony, having to be civil to him, pretend everything was fine... it was harder than I expected."

"Did he say anything to you? At the reception or during the ceremony?"

"At the reception, barely three words. But the way he looked at me..." Rebecca shuddered. "Like I'd personally wronged him by choosing Dennis. Like I owed him something after all these years. It was unsettling."

Mike whined softly, and Agatha reached down to stroke his head. "Rebecca, I need to ask—where were you during the tree lighting? When Paul was killed?"

Rebecca's expression closed off immediately. "I was there. At the ceremony. Like everyone else."

"Can you be more specific? Were you with Dennis? With anyone who could verify—"

"I was there," Rebecca repeated, her voice sharp. "In the square, watching the tree light up like everyone else. That's all I can tell you."

"You can't provide more details?"

"There were two hundred people there, Miss Royale. Everyone was moving around, watching the ceremony, talking to neighbors. I can't give you a minute-by-minute account of where I stood or who I spoke to." Rebecca's hands twisted in her lap. "Is that what you need? A perfect alibi? Well, I don't have one. Neither does Dennis. We were doing our jobs as mayor and first lady, being visible, being accessible. We weren't keeping track of every moment because we had no reason to think someone was being murdered."

The defensiveness in her tone suggested she'd given this same speech to Detective Dawson, probably multiple times.

"I'm not accusing you of anything," Agatha said gently. "I'm just trying to understand what happened."

"Then understand this: neither Dennis nor I killed Paul Chambers, despite having every emotional reason to wish him dead." Rebecca stood abruptly. "Now if you'll excuse me, I have to pick up some documents from the community center."

"Rebecca, wait." Agatha stood as well, Mike immediately alert beside her. "If you didn't kill Paul, then someone else did. Someone who had access to your knife, who knew about the history between you and Paul, who specifically wanted to frame Dennis."

"I know that." Rebecca's voice cracked slightly. "Don't

you think I know that? Someone was in our house, touching our things, taking that knife to use for murder. Someone wanted to destroy my husband, to destroy us. And they're succeeding."

"Then help me find out who."

"How? I don't know who took the knife. I don't know when it was taken. I didn't even notice it was missing until the police told us." Rebecca's composure was cracking, tears threatening. "I've tried to remember everyone who's been in our house recently, everyone who could have had access to the dining room where the knife was displayed. But we host so many events, so many people come through. It could have been anyone."

"The cleaning service?" Agatha suggested.

"They're bonded, background-checked, have been working for us for three years without any problems." Rebecca wiped at her eyes. "But yes, the police are investigating them too. Investigating everyone, apparently, except the actual killer."

"What about Paul? Had he been in your house recently?"

"God, no. We hadn't invited him anywhere in twenty years. The only reason we had to interact with him at all was because of his position as a judge. We couldn't avoid him at official county events, but we certainly didn't socialize with him." Rebecca took a shaky breath. "Seeing him at the reception was the first time I'd spoken to him in over a year."

Agatha tried a different approach. "Did Paul ever threaten you? Either of you? Try to use your past relationship against you in any way?"

Rebecca was quiet for a long moment. When she spoke,

her voice was barely above a whisper. "He made things difficult for Dennis professionally. Questioned his policies, filed complaints about minor issues, always seemed to be there when Dennis made a mistake, ready to publicize it. Was it because of me? Because I chose Dennis over him? I don't know. Paul never said explicitly. But the pattern was there."

"That must have been hard on your marriage."

"Dennis never blamed me. Not once." Rebecca's eyes filled with tears again. "He knew what Paul was, knew that Paul was petty and vindictive. He protected me from it as much as he could. And now..." Her voice broke. "Now everyone thinks he killed Paul because of me. Because of some ancient history that should have been buried decades ago."

Mike pressed against Agatha's leg, sensing the emotional tension. Agatha reached down to comfort him while studying Rebecca's face. The woman was clearly in pain, clearly frightened. But was she frightened because her husband was guilty? Or because she knew something—something she was desperately trying to protect?

"Rebecca, if you know anything that could help—"

"I don't." Rebecca's response was too quick, too defensive. "I've told you everything. I've told the police everything. Paul is dead, someone used our knife to kill him, and my husband is going to be arrested for murder despite being innocent. That's all I know."

She turned to leave, then paused, looking back at Agatha. "You solved other cases in Bristol Lake. People trust you. But don't waste your time trying to clear Dennis if you think he's guilty. And don't waste your time trying to investigate me.

We're victims in this, not perpetrators. Someone set us up, and they're watching us twist in the wind."

With that, she walked away, her elegant coat billowing in the cold December wind.

Agatha stood in the empty park with Mike, watching Rebecca disappear around the corner. The conversation had raised more questions than it answered. Rebecca admitted to hating Paul, but her hatred seemed rooted in old wounds rather than fresh rage. She couldn't provide an alibi, but that might simply mean she'd been absorbed in her mayoral duties during the ceremony. She was clearly hiding something, but whether that something was guilt or fear or simply a desperate attempt to protect her husband remained unclear.

"What do you think, Mike?" Agatha asked quietly. "Is she telling the truth?"

Mike tilted his head, his dark eyes unreadable.

The problem was, Agatha realized as they walked back toward the bookstore, that Rebecca was both believable and suspicious at the same time. Her pain seemed genuine, her fear real. But her evasiveness, her inability to provide specifics about her whereabouts, her obvious desperation to protect Dennis—all of it suggested she knew more than she was saying.

Was she protecting a guilty husband? Or was she protecting herself?

Or—and this was the possibility that kept nagging at Agatha—was she protecting someone else entirely? Someone who'd taken the knife, committed murder, and left the Crawfords to shoulder the blame?

Emma was waiting at the bookstore when Agatha

returned, her expression eager. "How did it go? Did Rebecca tell you anything?"

"She admitted to hating Paul. Said he cheated on her when they were engaged, that he was dishonest about many things." Agatha filled Emma in on the conversation while making them both tea. "But she wouldn't give details about where she was during the murder. Just kept saying she was 'there, at the ceremony, like everyone else.'"

"That's not much of an alibi."

"No, it's not." Agatha handed Emma a mug. "But here's what bothers me—she seemed genuinely afraid. Not guilty-afraid, but scared-for-her-life afraid. Like she knows something dangerous but can't or won't say what it is."

"You think she's protecting Dennis?"

"Maybe. Or maybe she's protecting herself." Agatha sipped her tea thoughtfully. "Or maybe there's something else going on that we're not seeing yet."

Emma pulled out her notebook. "I did some research at the library today. Found articles about restaurants Paul inspected. Villa Toscana Restaurant wasn't the only one to close—there were at least four others in the past two years. All claimed the violations were excessive or fabricated."

"Did any of them threaten Paul? File complaints?"

"One family filed a formal complaint with the county, but it was dismissed. Apparently Paul's record was too good, too many years of service. The county sided with him." Emma flipped through her notes. "But get this—I found something interesting about the Christmas tree competition. Three years ago, a town called Winthrop was disqualified after Paul discovered irregularities in their budget reporting.

They lost the competition and the grant money that came with it."

"Irregularities like what?"

"Falsified expense reports, something about padding costs to make the display seem more elaborate than it actually was. Paul caught it during his thorough review. The town was humiliated, the committee chair resigned in disgrace." Emma looked up. "Winthrop is only twenty miles from Bristol Lake. Several people from there attended the tree lighting ceremony."

Agatha felt a spark of interest. "Did you get names?"

"Working on it. The library has old programs from that competition. I'm going to see if I can match names to people who signed the attendance sheet at our ceremony." Emma grinned. "See? I'm learning from the best."

"You're learning to be nosy," Agatha said, but she smiled. "Good work, Emma. This gives us new leads to follow."

As Emma left to continue her research, Agatha sat in the quiet bookstore with Mike at her feet, staring at her notebook. They had suspects with secrets—Marina hiding something Paul discovered, Dennis and Rebecca with twenty years of resentment, people from Winthrop seeking revenge, families whose restaurants Paul had destroyed.

But they still didn't have the one thing that would crack the case open: proof of who'd taken the Crawford knife and used it to commit murder.

That knife was the key to everything. Not just the physical evidence, but the why and the how of it. Someone had deliberately chosen Dennis Crawford's distinctive Norwegian silver blade. Someone had planned this murder carefully enough to frame the mayor while committing it in the chaos of a public ceremony.

Who had that kind of access, that kind of motive, that kind of cold calculation?

And more importantly—were they finished? Or was framing Dennis just the beginning of something larger?

Agatha shivered despite the warmth of the bookstore, and Mike pressed closer to her leg as if sensing her unease.

Chapter 12

The Tourist's Video

Agatha was shelving books in the mystery section when her phone rang. Detective Dawson's name appeared on the screen.

"Agatha? Can you come to the station? Something's come up."

Twenty minutes later, she sat in Dawson's office with Mike at her feet. The detective looked both energized and troubled, a combination that usually meant a significant break in a case.

"A tourist came forward this morning," he said without preamble. "Family from Massachusetts who attended the tree lighting. The husband was recording the ceremony—you know how people do, capturing memories."

"And he caught something on video?"

"More than something." Dawson turned his laptop to face her. "He was reviewing the footage last night and noticed something odd. Thought he should bring it to us."

He pressed play. The video showed the town square after the tree lighting, the beautiful spruce glowing in the background. People milled about, some heading toward the cider station, others taking photographs. The timestamp in the corner read 7:52 PM—just minutes after the ceremony ended, before Paul's body had been discovered.

"Watch the right side of the frame," Dawson said quietly.

Agatha leaned forward, her eyes tracking the movement of various people in the crowd. Then she saw it—a figure in a burgundy coat moving purposefully toward one of the large trash bins near the gazebo.

Rebecca Crawford.

The video quality was surprisingly clear. Rebecca glanced around quickly—not furtively exactly, but checking to see if anyone was watching. Then she pulled something from her coat pocket and dropped it into the trash bin. The object was wrapped in what looked like a white cloth napkin, but its shape was unmistakable—long, slender, the distinctive outline of a knife.

Rebecca turned and walked away quickly, disappearing into the crowd.

The video ended.

Agatha sat back, her mind racing. "That's the knife. She threw away the murder weapon."

"That's what I thought too. The timestamp is right—7:52 PM, which is about twelve minutes after the tree lighting and eight minutes before you found Paul's body at eight o'clock." Dawson replayed the section. "The trash bin she used is one of the ones the cleaning crew emptied the next morning. The same crew that found the knife."

"So Rebecca disposed of the murder weapon." Agatha watched the video again, studying Rebecca's body language. "But why? If she killed Paul, why wait until after the ceremony to get rid of the knife? Why not leave it at the scene or take it home with her?"

"Good question." Dawson paused the video on a frame that clearly showed Rebecca's face. "We pulled the knife from evidence and checked for additional prints. Dennis's are all over the handle, as we knew. But we also found Rebecca's fingerprints—fresh ones, overlaying Dennis's in several places."

"She handled the knife recently."

"Very recently. Probably when she disposed of it." Dawson closed the laptop. "I've called Rebecca in for questioning. She's due here in thirty minutes."

Agatha stared at the blank laptop screen, trying to piece together what this meant. Rebecca had thrown away the knife that killed Paul Chambers. Her fingerprints were on it. She'd been seen on video disposing of evidence in a murder investigation.

It looked damning. Absolutely damning.

But something about it felt wrong.

"If Rebecca killed Paul," Agatha said slowly, "why would she use her own family knife? She had to know it would be traced back to them."

"People panic," Dawson said. "Make irrational decisions in the moment."

"But she didn't panic after the murder. She calmly attended the rest of the ceremony, stood beside Dennis while he gave speeches, smiled at constituents. Then, twelve minutes after the tree lighting, she deliberately walked to a trash bin and disposed of the weapon. That's not panic—that's calculation."

"Or it's someone who realizes she's made a terrible

mistake and is trying to cover it up." Dawson pulled out Rebecca's file. "Either way, she has a lot of explaining to do."

Mike whined softly at Agatha's feet. She reached down to stroke his head, her mind working through the timeline. The ceremony had ended around 7:40. Paul's body was discovered at 8:00. Rebecca had disposed of the knife at 7:52 —right in the middle of that twenty-minute window.

"Where was Rebecca when Paul was killed?" Agatha asked. "During the actual tree lighting, around 7:20 to 7:30?"

"She claims she was in the crowd, watching the ceremony like everyone else. No specific alibi." Dawson's expression was grim. "Which means she could have slipped away, killed Paul, and returned to the crowd. Then disposed of the weapon once the ceremony ended."

It was possible. Certainly possible. Rebecca had motive— twenty years of resentment toward the man who'd betrayed her. She had means—access to the knife in her own home. And opportunity—the chaos of the ceremony provided perfect cover.

But Agatha kept coming back to the same question: would Rebecca really be that foolish?

"What about Dennis?" she asked. "Does he know about this video yet?"

"No. I wanted to question Rebecca first, see her reaction." Dawson checked his watch. "She should be here any minute."

As if on cue, the desk sergeant knocked on the door. "Detective? Mrs. Crawford is here. She's in interview room two with her lawyer."

Dawson stood, gathering his files. "I need to handle this interview. But Agatha—" he hesitated. "I might need your

help afterward. Rebecca responds better to women, and you
have a way of getting people to open up. If the official interview doesn't yield results, would you be willing to try talking
to her? Unofficially?"

"Of course."

"Wait in the break room. This might take a while."

Agatha moved to the small break room with Mike,
accepting a cup of coffee from a sympathetic officer. Through
the window, she could see the interview room door—closed,
impenetrable. Behind it, Rebecca Crawford was about to face
evidence that made her look like a murderer.

Forty-five minutes passed. Then an hour. Agatha paced
the break room, Mike watching her with patient eyes. What
was taking so long? Had Rebecca confessed? Denied everything? Demanded a lawyer and refused to speak?

Finally, the interview room door opened. Rebecca
emerged first, her face ashen, her elegant composure
completely shattered. She looked like she might collapse at
any moment. Her lawyer—a woman Agatha didn't recognize
—supported her elbow, guiding her down the hallway.

Dawson appeared a moment later, his expression frustrated. He caught sight of Agatha and beckoned her into his
office.

"She won't talk," he said without preamble. "I showed her
the video, confronted her with the evidence, pointed out that
her fingerprints are on the murder weapon. She just sat there,
crying, refusing to explain."

"What did she say?"

"Only that she didn't kill Paul Chambers. When I asked
why she disposed of the knife, she went silent. When I asked
where she found it, silence. When I pointed out that obstruc-

tion of justice is a serious crime, she just kept crying."
Dawson slumped into his chair. "Her lawyer advised her not
to answer any questions that might incriminate her. So we're
at an impasse."

"Are you going to arrest her?"

"Not yet. But she's not allowed to leave town, and she
knows we're watching her." He rubbed his eyes. "Agatha, I
need you to try talking to her. Woman to woman, no official
capacity. See if you can get her to explain why she threw that
knife away."

"You think she'll talk to me?"

"I think she's terrified and desperate. Sometimes people
open up to civilians when they won't talk to police." Dawson
handed her a slip of paper with an address. "She's going
home now. Give her an hour to settle, then try. Please."

Agatha looked at the address—the Crawford house on
Elm Street, one of the nicest neighborhoods in Bristol Lake.

"I'll try," she said. "But Dawson—I don't think Rebecca
killed Paul."

"The evidence says otherwise."

"The evidence says she disposed of the murder weapon.
That's not the same thing as committing murder." Agatha
stood, Mike immediately alert beside her. "If Rebecca killed
Paul, why would she throw the knife in a public trash bin
where anyone might see her? Why not take it home and
dispose of it properly? Burn it, bury it, throw it in the
harbor?"

"You're assuming she was thinking clearly."

"I'm assuming she's not stupid." Agatha headed for the
door. "And everything about this case suggests careful planning, not panic. The knife, the timing, the location—someone

planned this murder very carefully. Throwing the weapon in a trash bin doesn't fit that pattern."

"Then why did she do it?"

That was the question, Agatha thought as she left the station with Mike. Why would Rebecca Crawford dispose of a murder weapon if she wasn't the murderer?

Only one answer made sense: she was protecting someone.

But who? Dennis, who'd been so desperate to keep her out of the investigation? Or someone else entirely?

The December sun hung low in the sky as Agatha walked toward Central Avenue, Mike trotting beside her. In one hour, she'd knock on Rebecca Crawford's door and ask questions that needed answers.

Until then, she'd do what she always did when faced with a puzzle: she'd think.

Because somewhere in the tangle of evidence and motives and secrets, there was a truth waiting to be uncovered.

And Agatha was determined to find it before an innocent woman went to prison for a crime she didn't commit.

If Rebecca was innocent, that is.

The video didn't lie. The fingerprints didn't lie.

But sometimes, the story they told wasn't the whole truth.

Chapter 13

The Confrontation

The Crawford house sat on a tree-lined street in Bristol Lake's most prestigious neighborhood—a elegant Colonial with white columns and a perfectly manicured lawn now dusted with snow. Christmas lights lined the roofline, and a wreath hung on the front door, festive touches that seemed almost obscene given the circumstances.

Agatha stood on the front porch with Mike beside her, gathering her courage before knocking. Through the window, she could see movement inside—Rebecca pacing across the living room, phone pressed to her ear, her posture rigid with tension.

Agatha knocked.

The movement inside stopped. A long pause followed, then footsteps approached. The door opened a crack, and Rebecca peered out, her face pale and drawn.

"Miss Royale." Her voice was flat, unwelcoming. "This isn't a good time."

"I know. I'm sorry to intrude. I was hoping we could talk for just a few minutes."

"I have nothing to say to you. Or to anyone." Rebecca started to close the door.

"Please," Agatha said quickly. "Just a few minutes. Not as part of any investigation. Just... one person trying to understand what happened to another."

Rebecca's hand paused on the door. For a moment, Agatha thought she'd refuse. Then she stepped back, opening the door wider.

"Five minutes. That's all."

The living room was beautifully decorated for Christmas—a tree in the corner laden with ornaments, garlands draped over the fireplace, the scent of pine and cinnamon in the air. But the warmth of the decorations contrasted sharply with the cold tension emanating from Rebecca.

She didn't offer Agatha a seat, didn't offer refreshments. Just stood in the center of the room with her arms crossed, a defensive posture that screamed "go away."

Mike sat at Agatha's feet, unusually still, as if sensing the hostility in the air.

"The video from the tourist," Agatha began carefully. "It shows you throwing something in the trash bin. Something that turned out to be the knife that killed Paul."

"I'm aware of what it shows." Rebecca's voice was brittle.

"Can you explain why you did that?"

"No."

"Rebecca, you could be charged with obstruction of justice. With tampering with evidence. With—"

"I'm aware of the charges I'm facing." Rebecca's eyes

flashed with something—anger? Fear? "My lawyer has explained them to me in great detail."

"Then help me understand. If you didn't kill Paul—"

"I didn't."

"Then why dispose of the murder weapon? Where did you find it? Why didn't you call the police immediately?"

Rebecca turned away, walking to the window that overlooked her snow-covered garden. "I can't answer those questions."

"Can't or won't?"

"Does it matter?" Rebecca's shoulders tensed. "The result is the same. I'm not going to explain my actions to you or to anyone else."

Agatha tried a different approach. "Were you protecting someone?"

Rebecca spun around, her expression sharp. "Who would I be protecting?"

"Dennis? Your husband was terrified during questioning. If you thought he was involved—"

"I'm not discussing my husband with you." Rebecca's voice rose slightly. "Dennis has nothing to do with this."

"But the knife was yours. From your house. Your fingerprints are on it along with his. You disposed of it after Paul was killed. How can Dennis have nothing to do with it?"

"Because he doesn't!" Rebecca's control was cracking, her voice shaking. "Why can't anyone believe that we didn't do this? That we're victims in this, not perpetrators?"

"Then tell me what happened. Help me understand—"

"I can't." Rebecca's voice broke. "I can't tell you anything. Don't you understand? I can't."

"Why not?"

Silence. Rebecca stared at her, tears streaming down her face, but her lips pressed together in a firm line.

"Rebecca, if you're innocent—"

"If?" Rebecca laughed, a harsh sound. "Everyone's already decided I'm guilty. The video, the fingerprints, the motive. It doesn't matter what I say. No one will believe me anyway."

"I might believe you," Agatha said quietly. "If you give me a reason to."

Rebecca wiped at her tears, her expression hardening. "I think you should leave now, Miss Royale."

"Please—"

"Leave. Now." Rebecca walked to the door and opened it, cold December air rushing in. "I won't be answering any more questions. Not from you, not from Detective Dawson, not from anyone without my lawyer present. Is that clear?"

Agatha had no choice but to comply. She walked to the door with Mike, pausing on the threshold. "Rebecca, if you're protecting someone, you need to know—you could go to prison for this. Is that person worth sacrificing your freedom for?"

Rebecca's expression was unreadable. "Goodbye, Miss Royale."

The door closed with finality.

Agatha stood on the porch for a moment, her mind churning. That conversation had gone nowhere—worse than nowhere. Rebecca had been defensive, evasive, almost hostile. She'd admitted nothing, explained nothing, and her refusal to provide any information made her look even more guilty than before.

Had Agatha been wrong? Was Rebecca actually the killer, and all her protestations of innocence were just lies?

Mike whined softly, pressing against her leg. Agatha reached down to scratch his ears, feeling the familiar frustration of a puzzle with missing pieces.

She walked back toward Central Avenue slowly, trying to sort through what she'd just witnessed. Rebecca's fear had seemed genuine—but fear of what? Prosecution for murder? Or something else?

The afternoon sun cast long shadows across the snow as Agatha reached the commercial district. Despite the murder investigation, despite the pall it had cast over the town, Bristol Lake was still preparing for Christmas. Shop windows glowed with festive displays, garlands decorated every lamppost, and the sounds of carols drifted from various storefronts.

People carried shopping bags laden with gifts, stopped to chat with neighbors, examined window displays of toys and books and jewelry. The hardware store had a display of sleds and ice skates. The pharmacy window featured an elaborate gingerbread village. And Eliza's Cottage Bakery had a line out the door, people waiting for Christmas cookies and holiday breads.

Life went on, Agatha thought. Even with a murderer walking among them, even with uncertainty and suspicion in the air, Bristol Lake continued its Christmas preparations. There was something both reassuring and unsettling about that—the resilience of community, but also the way tragedy could be absorbed and almost normalized.

"Agatha!" Emma waved from outside the library, her arms full of books. "Are you heading back to the bookstore?"

"Eventually." Agatha crossed the street to join her friend.

"Just finished talking to Rebecca Crawford. Or trying to, anyway."

"And?" Emma's eyes were bright with curiosity behind her tortoiseshell glasses.

"She wouldn't tell me anything. Refused to explain why she threw away the knife, wouldn't say where she found it, just kept insisting she's innocent but won't provide any proof."

"That doesn't sound good."

"No, it doesn't." Agatha fell into step beside Emma as they walked toward One Deadly Chapter. The bookstore window was decorated with a display of Christmas mysteries —appropriate, given the circumstances. "She seemed terrified, Emma. But whether she's terrified because she's guilty or because she's being framed, I honestly can't tell."

"What does Detective Dawson think?"

"That the evidence speaks for itself. Video footage, fingerprints, motive, opportunity. It all points to Rebecca." Agatha unlocked the bookstore door, and they stepped into the warmth. "But something still feels wrong about it."

"Your instincts?"

"My instincts say Rebecca is hiding something important. But I don't know if that something is murder or something else entirely."

They settled into the café area, Mike curling up in his favorite spot near the fireplace. Emma set down her stack of books—Christmas-themed fiction for the library's holiday display—and pulled out her notebook.

"I've been doing more research," she said. "About Paul's work as a health inspector. There are at least six restaurants that closed after his inspections in the past three years. Six families who lost their businesses, their livelihoods, everything."

"That's a lot of potential suspects."

"And I found something interesting about one of them." Emma flipped through her notes. "Villa Toscana Restaurant in Petunia Heights. Beautiful Italian place, family-owned for two generations. Paul shut them down two years ago. The owner, Anthony Greene, died six months later—heart attack, according to the obituary, but his widow claimed it was a broken heart."

"That's tragic."

"It is. And the daughter—Larissa Greene—had to drop out of college to help support the family. The mother now works as a house cleaner." Emma looked up. "Imagine losing everything because one inspector decided your restaurant didn't meet his standards. Standards that other people said were excessive and unfair."

Agatha made a note of the name. Villa Toscana Restaurant. She'd heard it mentioned before—Gladys had talked about the excellent food, Lorraine had referenced it as an example of Paul's strictness. Another family destroyed by Paul Chambers's thoroughness.

"It's starting to look like half the county had a motive to kill Paul," Agatha said.

"That's what makes this so difficult. The Crawfords are obvious suspects because of the knife and their personal history with Paul. But what if someone else killed him specifically to frame them? Someone who had access to their house, knew about their grudge against Paul, and used that knowledge to point suspicion in their direction?"

It was a theory Agatha had considered. But proving it

would require finding that someone—a needle in a haystack of potential suspects.

Her phone buzzed with a text from Detective Dawson: *Marina Hawkins has agreed to explain her alibi. Coming in tomorrow morning at 9. Thought you'd want to know.*

Agatha showed the text to Emma.

"Finally," Emma said. "Maybe she'll clear up whatever secret Paul was threatening to expose."

"And maybe," Agatha added, "she'll give us information that points away from Rebecca and toward the real killer."

If Rebecca was innocent, that is.

Agatha still wasn't sure.

The afternoon wore on, and customers began trickling into the bookstore—people looking for last-minute gifts, seeking recommendations for holiday reading, wanting the comfort of books and community in uncertain times. Agatha helped them find mysteries and thrillers, suggested cozy reads perfect for snowy evenings, wrapped purchases in festive paper.

It was almost possible to forget about murder, about knives in trash bins, about a woman who refused to explain her suspicious actions.

Almost.

But as the winter darkness fell early and the Christmas lights along Central Avenue began to glow, Agatha couldn't shake the image of Rebecca's face—terrified and defiant in equal measure, protecting a secret she wouldn't share.

Tomorrow, Marina would explain her alibi, and perhaps that would clear one suspect and narrow the field.

But tonight, Agatha locked up the bookstore with more questions than answers.

Rebecca Crawford had disposed of a murder weapon. The video proved it. The fingerprints confirmed it.

But was she a killer? Or was she something else—a frightened woman protecting a secret that might destroy more than just herself?

Agatha walked home through the decorated streets with Mike trotting beside her, the cheerful Christmas lights casting long shadows on the snow.

Somewhere in Bristol Lake, a killer was watching the investigation unfold. Watching Rebecca take the blame. Watching Dennis twist in the wind of suspicion.

And feeling, perhaps, very confident that they'd gotten away with murder.

But Agatha had learned one thing over the years: confidence bred carelessness.

And when the killer made their mistake—and they would, eventually—she intended to be watching.

Tomorrow, Marina's story. Then, piece by piece, the truth would emerge.

It had to.

Because if Rebecca Crawford went to prison for a crime she didn't commit, justice wouldn't just be delayed.

It would be dead.

Chapter 14

Marina's Alibi

Agatha was helping a customer find a Christie novel when the bell above the door chimed. Marina Hawkins entered, looking considerably better than the last time Agatha had seen her—still nervous, but more composed, as if a weight had been lifted.

"Miss Royale," Marina said hesitantly. "I hope I'm not interrupting. I was hoping to find something to read. Something... distracting."

"Of course." Agatha finished with her customer and gestured toward the classic mystery section. "We have an excellent selection. Are you looking for anything in particular?"

"Something with a happy ending," Marina said with a weak smile. "I could use some reassurance that justice prevails."

Mike trotted over to greet Marina, tail wagging. She bent down to pet him, and some of the tension seemed to ease from her shoulders.

Emma emerged from the back room with a stack of books

for restocking. "Marina! I heard you were at the police station this morning." Her tone was friendly, curious rather than accusatory. "Is everything all right?"

Marina straightened, color rising in her cheeks. "Yes, actually. I finally explained everything to Detective Dawson. I should have been honest from the beginning."

Lorraine swept in from the café area, carrying a cup of coffee. "Ah, Marina! The judge from Camden, non? I have been hearing your name mentioned quite a bit these past days."

"All bad things, I'm sure," Marina said quietly.

"Not at all!" Lorraine settled into one of the café chairs. "People are very curious, that is true. But curious is not the same as condemning."

Agatha brought Marina a cup of tea and guided her to the café table. Sometimes the best interrogations didn't feel like interrogations at all—just friendly conversations in comfortable settings.

"I'm glad you spoke with Detective Dawson," Agatha said carefully. "He mentioned you were coming in. Did you... were you able to clear things up?"

Marina wrapped her hands around the warm cup. "Yes. I told him where I really was during the murder. I should have told him days ago, but I was so embarrassed."

"Where were you?" Emma asked, joining them at the table with her own coffee.

Marina took a deep breath. "I was sitting on a bench at the back of the town square, near Maple Street. I was with someone—my boyfriend, Michael Reeves."

"A boyfriend!" Lorraine's eyes lit up. "How romantic! But why would this be something to hide?"

"Because I just got divorced six months ago," Marina explained, her words coming faster now. "And Michael is younger than me—twelve years younger. We work together on the judging circuit, and people might think it's inappropriate. We've only been seeing each other for three months, and we weren't ready to go public yet."

"So when you were both at the tree lighting..." Agatha prompted gently.

"We decided to watch from a distance. Together, but not obviously together. We sat on that bench from about seven o'clock until after eight, when we heard the commotion about Paul's body." Marina's relief at finally sharing this was evident. "Michael can confirm it—he already has, to Detective Dawson. And there were other people nearby who saw us. A couple with young children, some teenagers hanging out near Maple Street."

Emma pulled out her ever-present notebook. "So you have an alibi. That's good!"

"Yes." Marina sipped her tea. "Detective Dawson verified it this morning. Called Michael, contacted the witnesses. It all checks out."

"Then why did you look so nervous around Paul?" Agatha asked. "At the reception, during the ceremony—you were clearly uncomfortable."

Marina's expression darkened. "Because Paul had discovered something about me. Something that could ruin my career."

"Oh là là!" Lorraine leaned forward dramatically. "A secret!"

"Not a terrible secret, but... unethical." Marina set down her cup. "Paul found out that I've been accepting gifts from towns I judge. Not bribes—nothing that influenced my scores. Just tokens of appreciation. A gift basket, a nice dinner, sometimes a small donation to a charity I support. Many judges accept small courtesies like this."

"But Paul did not approve?" Lorraine asked.

"Paul was adamant that it was unethical, that it created the appearance of impropriety. He threatened to expose me—file a formal complaint with the judging committee, document every gift I'd accepted, make it all public." Marina's voice dropped. "I would have been disqualified from judging, probably banned from the circuit entirely. My reputation would be destroyed."

"That's why you were so nervous," Agatha said, understanding dawning. "And when Paul died—"

"I panicked," Marina admitted. "I had a clear motive for wanting him silenced. I was terrified you'd all think I killed him. That's why I tried to leave town, which was incredibly stupid. I should have just been honest about where I was and who I was with."

"But you were afraid of the relationship becoming public," Emma said sympathetically.

"Yes. And I thought if I admitted I was with Michael, no one would believe me. They'd think I was making up an alibi." Marina looked at each of them in turn. "I know it sounds ridiculous now. But in the moment, with Paul dead and everyone asking questions, I just... froze."

Agatha studied Marina carefully. The woman's embarrassment seemed genuine, her relief at finally telling the truth palpable. And an alibi with multiple witnesses was difficult to fake.

"What did Paul threaten exactly?" Agatha asked. "When did he plan to expose you?"

"He gave me until the end of the year to resign from the judging circuit voluntarily. If I didn't, he said he'd file his complaint in January." Marina's hands trembled slightly. "That's why I kept checking my phone at the tree lighting. I was texting Michael, asking for advice, trying to figure out what to do."

"How did Paul discover your... gift accepting?" Emma asked.

"I don't know exactly. He was very thorough in his investigations—not just about judging, but everything. He probably noticed I was dining at expensive restaurants in towns I'd judged, or maybe someone mentioned the gifts to him. Once Paul suspected something, he was relentless in finding proof." Marina shook her head. "He prided himself on his thoroughness."

"That thoroughness must have made him many enemies," Lorraine observed.

"It did," Marina agreed. "In his work as a health inspector too. He shut down several restaurants, always very strict with violations. Some people thought he was too harsh, that he used his position to... well, to punish people who didn't cooperate with him."

This aligned with what Agatha had been learning about Paul—a man who wielded his authority like a weapon, who collected secrets and used them for leverage.

"But you didn't kill him," Agatha said. It wasn't a question.

"No. I couldn't have—I was with Michael the entire time. Detective Dawson verified it this morning." Marina's relief was evident. "I may face consequences for accepting those gifts, and my judging career might be over, but at least I won't be facing murder charges."

After Marina selected a few books and left—looking considerably lighter than when she'd arrived—Emma, Lorraine, and Agatha remained at the café table.

"Well," Emma said, making notes. "That eliminates Marina as a suspect."

"She could not have done it," Lorraine agreed. "Not with a boyfriend and witnesses to confirm she was elsewhere. This alibi is—how do you say—solid."

"Which brings us back to the Crawfords," Agatha said, frustration creeping into her voice. "Rebecca disposing of the murder weapon, Dennis with his vague alibi and twenty-year grudge."

"Or someone else entirely," Emma suggested. "Someone we haven't identified yet."

"If there is someone else, they're very good at staying hidden," Agatha said. She pulled out her notebook, reviewing her list of suspects. Patricia Anderson and Robert Coleman had solid alibis. Marina now had one too. That left Dennis and Rebecca Crawford, both with motive, means, and no credible alibis.

The circle was narrowing to an uncomfortable conclusion.

"The evidence seems overwhelming," Emma said quietly. "Against the Crawfords, I mean."

"Almost too overwhelming," Agatha murmured. "If Dennis or Rebecca killed Paul, why use a distinctive family heirloom that points directly back to them? Why dispose of it in a public trash bin where anyone might see?"

"Perhaps they panicked?" Lorraine suggested. "Made foolish decisions in the moment?"

"Maybe." But Agatha's instincts said otherwise. The more she learned about this case, the more calculated it seemed. The knife, the timing, the location—someone had planned this carefully.

And yet the knife disposal suggested panic or carelessness.

The two things didn't fit together.

"We're missing something," Agatha said finally. "Something important."

"Then we must find it," Lorraine declared. "And quickly, before poor Rebecca is arrested for a crime she did not commit!"

"Do you really think she's innocent?" Emma asked. "After everything—the video, the fingerprints, the motive?"

"I think the evidence is convenient," Agatha said carefully. "Maybe too convenient. Someone wanted the Crawfords to look guilty."

"Then we must find out who," Lorraine said firmly.

Agatha looked at her friends, at their determined expressions, and felt grateful for their support. "We start by investigating everyone who had access to the Crawford house in the past month. And we find out who else had a reason to want Paul Chambers dead—and Dennis Crawford blamed for it."

"Where exactly do we start?" Emma asked, pen poised over her notebook.

Agatha flipped through her notes, reviewing everything they'd learned. "We start by following the knife. Someone took it from the Crawford house. We need to know who had the opportunity."

It wouldn't be easy. But then again, nothing about this case had been easy from the start.

The killer had been clever, careful, calculating. They'd framed the perfect suspects, created the perfect misdirection.

But no one was perfect. Eventually, they'd slip up.

And when they did, Agatha would be watching.

Mike stretched at her feet and yawned, oblivious to the complexities of human deception. Agatha reached down to scratch his ears, drawing comfort from his simple, honest presence.

Somewhere in Bristol Lake, a killer was walking free, watching the investigation close in on the wrong suspects, feeling confident they'd gotten away with murder.

But confidence bred carelessness.

And Agatha had learned one thing over the years: the truth always found a way to surface.

Even when it was buried under layers of lies.

Chapter 15

Dennis's Discovery

Agatha couldn't sleep that night. She lay in bed, staring at the ceiling while Mike snored softly at the foot of the bed. Something about the timeline kept nagging at her—a detail that didn't quite fit.

Rebecca had disposed of the knife at 7:52 PM, according to the tourist's video. That was twelve minutes after the tree lighting ended, and eight minutes before Agatha discovered Paul's body at 8:00 PM.

But Paul had been killed during the tree lighting itself, around 7:20 to 7:30. Which meant the knife had been lying beside his body for at least twenty minutes before Rebecca threw it in the trash.

How had Rebecca found it during those twenty minutes? The body was hidden behind the tree stand platform, not visible from the crowd. Paul had been missing, yes, but no one knew he was dead yet. No one had reason to search behind the platform.

Except...

Agatha sat up suddenly, her mind racing. Dennis had

noticed Paul step away before the tree lighting. Multiple witnesses confirmed he'd seemed distracted during the ceremony, tense, preoccupied.

What if Dennis had gone looking for Paul?

What if Dennis had found the body—and the knife—before anyone else?

The pieces clicked into place with sudden clarity. Dennis finding Paul dead, recognizing the distinctive Norwegian silver knife immediately. Panicking. And then... what? Had he told Rebecca? Had she gone back to dispose of it?

Or had Dennis himself moved the knife, and Rebecca discovered what he'd done?

Agatha got out of bed, startling Mike awake. "Come on, boy. We need to talk to Emma."

Twenty minutes later, Emma arrived at Agatha's house in her pajamas and winter coat, her red hair in a messy ponytail. "This had better be important. I was having a very nice dream about a library that never ran out of funding."

Agatha made tea and explained her theory. Emma listened, her expression shifting from sleepy confusion to alert understanding.

"So you think Dennis found the body first, saw his own knife, and just... left it there?"

"I think he panicked. Saw his family heirloom lying beside a man he'd publicly hated, realized how it would look, and fled." Agatha paced her kitchen. "But then something happened with Rebecca. Either he told her, or she discovered it somehow. And she ended up disposing of the knife."

"That's obstruction of justice. For both of them."

"I know. But it would explain their behavior—the terror, the evasiveness, the way they keep protecting each other." Agatha sat down across from Emma. "We need to talk to Dennis. Get him to admit what really happened."

"He wouldn't talk to you last time."

"Last time, I was asking if he killed Paul. This time, I'm asking what he saw when he found the body." Agatha pulled out her phone. "That's a very different question."

DENNIS CRAWFORD AGREED to meet Agatha at his office early the next morning, though he sounded wary on the phone. When she arrived with Emma—she'd insisted on having a witness—he looked even worse than before. His office was a mess of papers and cold coffee cups, suggesting he hadn't been sleeping much either.

"Miss Royale. Miss Fletcher." He gestured to chairs but didn't sit himself, instead standing by the window over-looking the town square. From here, you could see the Christmas tree, still lit, still beautiful, still tainted by death. "What is this about?"

"About what you saw," Agatha said simply. "When you found Paul's body."

Dennis went rigid. "I didn't—"

"You did," Agatha interrupted gently. "You noticed Paul step away before the tree lighting. You were distracted during the ceremony—several people mentioned it. And at some point, you went looking for him."

Dennis turned from the window, his face pale. "I don't know what you're talking about."

"I think you do. I think you went behind the tree stand platform sometime between 7:30 and 7:40, and you found Paul dead. With your family's Norwegian silver knife lying beside him."

The silence stretched out. Dennis's hands clenched and unclenched at his sides.

"You panicked," Agatha continued quietly. "Anyone would have. Your worst enemy dead, killed with your own distinctive knife. You knew how it would look. So you left without reporting it."

"This is speculation," Dennis said, but his voice shook.

"Is it?" Emma asked. "Because it explains everything— your terror during questioning, your refusal to explain where you were, the way you kept insisting Rebecca had nothing to do with it."

"Rebecca didn't kill him," Dennis said quickly. Too quickly.

"We know," Agatha said. "But what happened after you found the body? Did you tell Rebecca?"

Dennis sank into his chair, all pretense crumbling. He looked like a man who'd been carrying an impossible weight and could no longer hold it up.

"How did you know?" he whispered.

"The timeline," Agatha explained. "Someone had to have found the body between 7:30 and 7:52—someone who knew where to look. You were the only person who made sense."

Dennis put his head in his hands. "I did go looking for him. Not because I wanted to confront him—I just... I saw him go behind the tree stand, and he didn't come back. It had been ten or fifteen minutes. I was worried he was back there judging the tree from different angles, finding flaws, preparing to give us a low score out of spite."

"What did you find?" Emma asked softly.

"Paul. On the ground. Dead." Dennis's voice was hollow. "And that knife—my grandmother's knife—lying right beside him. I recognized it immediately. I've seen it in our dining room cabinet my entire life."

"What did you do?"

"I froze. Just stood there staring. All I could think was 'this is a setup.' Someone killed Paul with our knife to frame Rebecca or me. Maybe both of us." Dennis looked up, his eyes red. "I should have called for help immediately. I know that. But I panicked. I thought if I reported it, if anyone knew I'd been there, found the body—it would look even worse."

"So you left," Agatha said.

"I left. Went back to the ceremony, tried to act normal, tried to smile and greet people while my mind was screaming." Dennis's hands trembled. "I couldn't think straight. I couldn't process what I'd seen."

"Did you tell Rebecca?" Agatha asked carefully.

Dennis hesitated, his expression conflicted. "I... yes. After the ceremony ended, after the crowd started dispersing. She could tell something was terribly wrong. I told her what I'd found."

"And what did she do?"

"She said she needed to see for herself. To confirm it was real, that I hadn't been mistaken." Dennis's voice dropped. "She went to look."

"And she found the knife," Emma said.

Dennis's hands clenched on the desk. "She came back

and said... said the body was there, but the knife was gone. Someone must have taken it already."

Agatha frowned. This didn't match the video evidence at all. "But the tourist's video shows Rebecca throwing the knife in the trash at 7:52. If it was already gone when she went to look—"

"Maybe she was mistaken. Maybe in the dark, the confusion—" Dennis was fumbling now, his story falling apart. "It was chaotic. People everywhere. Maybe she didn't see it."

"Dennis," Agatha said carefully, "we have video evidence of Rebecca disposing of the knife. Clear video. There's no mistake."

"Then I don't know." Dennis wouldn't meet their eyes. "Maybe she saw something else. Maybe she found it somewhere else. You'd have to ask her what she saw."

"We're asking you," Emma pressed. "What exactly did Rebecca tell you when she came back?"

"That the body was there. That Paul was dead. That we needed to be careful, that someone was trying to frame us." Dennis's voice was unconvincing even to his own ears. "That's what she told me."

"But not about the knife?" Agatha asked. "She didn't mention finding the knife and throwing it away?"

"No. I mean—" Dennis ran his hands through his hair. "I don't remember exactly what she said. It was all so overwhelming. Maybe she did mention the knife. I can't recall every detail."

The lies were transparent now. Dennis was protecting Rebecca, but his story had too many holes, too many contradictions.

"Dennis," Agatha said quietly, "you're not helping

Rebecca by lying. The video evidence is clear. She disposed of the murder weapon. We need to know why."

"I don't know why!" Dennis's control cracked. "I told you what I know. I found the body, I told Rebecca, and after that —" He stopped abruptly. "After that, everything's confused. I can't give you a clear timeline. I can't tell you exactly what Rebecca did or didn't do."

"Can't or won't?" Emma asked.

Dennis stood abruptly, turning back to the window. "I think this conversation is over. If you want to know what Rebecca did, ask her. I've told you everything I can."

But he hadn't. That much was obvious. Dennis was protecting Rebecca, lying about her involvement, trying to shield her from something.

The question was: what was he protecting her from? Murder? Or just the consequences of disposing of evidence?

Agatha stood, signaling Emma to do the same. "Dennis, you need to tell Detective Dawson the truth. All of it. About finding the body, about what you told Rebecca, about what really happened."

"I'll consider it," Dennis said, but his tone suggested he wouldn't.

"If you don't, Rebecca will face the consequences alone," Agatha warned. "Is that what you want?"

Dennis's shoulders sagged. "Of course not. But I..." He trailed off, unable to finish.

"Talk to your lawyer," Emma suggested gently. "Figure out the best way to come forward. But do it soon, before this gets any worse."

They left Dennis standing at his window, staring out at the Christmas tree where his life had begun to unravel.

OUTSIDE, Emma pulled her coat tighter against the cold. "He's lying. About Rebecca, I mean."

"Obviously," Agatha agreed. "The question is why. What is he protecting her from?"

"Maybe he thinks she killed Paul," Emma said slowly. "He found the body, told her, and then she went back and... finished what she'd started? Or cleaned up evidence?"

"Or maybe he's just a terrified man trying to protect his wife from a murder charge, even if it means his story doesn't make sense." Agatha shook her head. "Either way, his lies are making them both look guilty."

They walked slowly down Central Avenue, the December morning bright and cold. Christmas decorations glittered in the sunlight, cheerful and incongruous given the darkness of their conversation.

"So what do we know for certain?" Emma pulled out her notebook. "Dennis found the body between 7:30 and 7:40. The knife was there. He left without reporting it. Rebecca threw the knife in the trash at 7:52. But Dennis's story about what Rebecca did doesn't match the evidence."

"Which means either Dennis is lying to protect Rebecca, or..." Agatha trailed off, uncomfortable with where that thought led.

"Or one of them really did kill Paul," Emma finished quietly. "Maybe it wasn't premeditated. Maybe Rebecca brought the knife to the ceremony for some innocent reason— cutting cake, or it was in her purse for some other purpose. And then she saw Paul, twenty years of resentment bubbled up, and she just... snapped."

"Or Dennis did," Agatha said. "Went to confront Paul, brought the knife without really thinking about what he was doing, and things escalated."

"And now they're protecting each other because they love each other," Emma added. "He found the body because he's the one who created it. Or she disposed of the weapon she used herself."

Agatha felt a chill that had nothing to do with the December cold. "I keep wanting to believe they were framed. That someone else took their knife, killed Paul, and set them up. It feels too convenient, too perfect."

"But maybe sometimes the obvious answer is the right answer," Emma said gently. "You always say that in mystery novels, the clever twist is satisfying. But in real life, people kill for simple reasons—rage, resentment, revenge. And then they panic and make mistakes trying to cover it up."

"I know." Agatha looked up at the Christmas tree visible from where they stood. "The evidence is overwhelming. Their knife, their motive, their opportunity, their lies. What kind of fool am I to doubt it?"

"You're not a fool. You're thorough," Emma said. "But Agatha... what if this time, the evidence is right? What if Dennis or Rebecca—or both of them—really did kill Paul?"

Agatha didn't answer for a long moment. Mike pressed against her leg, sensing her troubled thoughts.

"Then we need to find proof," she said finally. "One way or the other. Either proof that they're guilty, or proof that someone else had access to that knife and used it to frame them."

"How do we do that?"

"We keep digging. We find out who else had access to the

Crawford house. We look at everyone Paul hurt, everyone who might want him dead." Agatha pulled her coat tighter. "And we follow the evidence, even if it leads somewhere I don't want it to go."

"What if it leads to Rebecca?" Emma asked quietly. "Or Dennis?"

"Then we accept it." Agatha's voice was heavy. "But until I'm absolutely certain, until every other possibility is exhausted, I'm going to keep looking."

Because the alternative—that she'd been wrong, that her instincts had failed her, that Dennis and Rebecca really were cold-blooded killers—was too terrible to accept without absolute proof.

But as she walked back toward her bookstore with Mike trotting beside her, doubt gnawed at her.

What if Emma was right? What if the obvious answer was the correct one?

What if she was protecting murderers instead of helping victims?

The uncertainty settled in her stomach like a stone, heavy and cold.

She'd know soon enough.

One way or another, the truth would surface.

She just wasn't sure anymore which truth she'd find.

Chapter 16

Loretta Thornton

The bell above the bookstore door chimed, and a woman swept in with all the dramatic flair of a stage actress making an entrance. She was in her fifties, dressed in a long black coat with a fur collar, her hair styled in elaborate waves, her makeup slightly too heavy for daytime. She paused just inside the door, one hand pressed to her chest, surveying the bookstore as if she'd entered a cathedral.

Mike, lying by the fireplace, lifted his head with mild interest, then settled back down. Apparently, even dramatic entrances didn't warrant getting up on a Tuesday afternoon.

"Oh!" the woman breathed, her voice carrying across the quiet shop. "How charming! How absolutely perfect! Paul would have loved this place. He adored mysteries, you know. Simply adored them."

Agatha looked up from the register where she'd been processing an order. "Can I help you find something?"

"I'm not here to shop, though I should, I really should. Paul always said I didn't read enough." The woman dabbed at her eyes with a lace handkerchief that appeared from nowhere. "I'm Loretta Thornton. Paul Chambers was my cousin. My dear, dear cousin."

"Oh." Agatha came around the counter. "I'm so sorry for your loss."

"It's devastating. Simply devastating." Loretta pressed the handkerchief to her nose. "I came as soon as I heard. Someone had to handle the arrangements, and Paul had no one else. No wife, no children, no siblings. Just me." She said this with a mixture of sorrow and pride, as if being Paul's only relative elevated her importance.

"Are you staying in town?"

"At the Harborside Inn. Charming place, though the mattress is rather firm." Loretta drifted toward the mystery section, running her fingers along the spines. "I've been speaking with the funeral home, making arrangements. Paul deserves a proper service. Something dignified. He was such an important man, you know. County health inspector, respected judge. People relied on his expertise."

Agatha noted the way Loretta spoke of Paul—all glowing praise, no mention of his strictness or the enemies he'd made. Either she was genuinely oblivious to her cousin's darker side, or she was deliberately painting him as a saint.

"I'm sure you're very busy with all the arrangements," Agatha said carefully. "But if you need any recommendations for restaurants or services—"

"Oh, I'm managing. Though it's all so overwhelming!" Loretta turned suddenly, fixing Agatha with an intense gaze. "You found him, didn't you? You and your little dog. I heard all about it."

"Yes. I'm sorry—"

"No, no, don't apologize! You did a service, really. Better you than some stranger." Loretta moved closer, lowering her voice conspiratorially. "Between you and me, I think it was the mayor. Dennis Crawford. Everyone says they hated each other. Twenty years of bad blood! And then his knife—his own family knife—used to kill poor Paul. It's obvious, isn't it?"

"The police are investigating," Agatha said neutrally.

"Oh, investigating." Loretta waved this away. "I've been reading mystery novels all week—research, you might say— and it's always the obvious suspect who did it. The one with motive and means and opportunity. That's the mayor, clear as day."

Before Agatha could respond, Lorraine entered from the café area, carrying a tray of fresh coffee. Her eyes widened slightly at the sight of Loretta's dramatic appearance, but her smile was warm.

"Bonjour! A new customer! Would you like some coffee? Fresh from the pot, très délicieux."

"How kind! Yes, please." Loretta accepted a cup with a gracious nod. "Are you the owner's friend?"

"I am Lorraine Dubois, and I am everyone's friend!" Lorraine settled into one of the café chairs, clearly intrigued by this theatrical newcomer. "And you are?"

"Loretta Thornton. Paul Chambers was my cousin." The handkerchief reappeared. "My dear, departed cousin."

"Ah! My condolences." Lorraine's expression turned sympathetic. "You must be devastated."

"I am. Simply devastated. Paul was all I had." Loretta sank into a chair, somehow making even sitting down look dramatic. "We weren't close—he was a private person, you understand—but family is family. And now I'm left to handle everything. His estate, his affairs, his poor empty house in Petunia Heights."

Agatha's ears perked up at that. "You're his heir?"

"His only living relative, so yes, I suppose I am. Not that there's much to inherit—Paul wasn't wealthy. But his house, his savings, a few investments. It all comes to me now." Loretta sipped her coffee. "I don't want it, of course. I'd rather have my cousin back."

The words were appropriate, but something in Loretta's tone suggested she wasn't entirely unhappy about the inheritance.

"You must stay in Bristol Lake for a while, non?" Lorraine asked. "For the funeral arrangements?"

"A few more days at least. The police want me available for questions, though I've told them everything I know. Which is nothing, really. I wasn't even in town when it happened." Loretta's voice turned excited, as if relishing her role in the drama. "I was in Portland, visiting friends. Didn't hear about Paul's death until the next morning."

"You didn't attend the tree lighting ceremony?" Agatha asked.

"No, no. I had plans in Portland that night." Loretta waved vaguely. "Though I wish I had been here. Maybe I could have prevented it somehow. Warned Paul. Protected him."

Over the next hour, as Loretta lingered in the bookstore— examining mysteries, asking questions about Bristol Lake, and periodically dabbing at her eyes—a pattern emerged. She was dramatic, theatrical, and seemed to genuinely grieve

Paul. But she also clearly enjoyed being at the center of the tragedy, being important, being noticed.

THE NEXT MORNING, Loretta appeared at the bookstore again.

"I've been thinking," she announced without preamble, "and I believe I was wrong about the mayor."

Agatha looked up from helping a customer. "Oh?"

"Yes. I think it was that judge—Marina Hawkins. Paul mentioned her to me once, said she was cutting corners, not following proper procedures. He was planning to report her!" Loretta's eyes gleamed with the thrill of conspiracy. "She had every reason to want him silenced."

"Marina has an alibi," Agatha said carefully, not mentioning that she'd learned this directly from Marina herself.

"Alibis can be faked," Loretta insisted. "In mystery novels, the killer always has an alibi. That's how you know they did it!"

Emma, who was restocking shelves nearby, caught Agatha's eye and suppressed a smile.

"I'll keep that in mind," Agatha said diplomatically.

ON THE THIRD day of Loretta's visits, she had a new theory.

"Rebecca Crawford," she declared, setting her purse down with emphasis. "It has to be Rebecca. Paul jilted her, you know. Or she jilted him—I forget which. But there was bad blood. A woman scorned and all that."

"I thought you said it was the mayor," Emma reminded her.

"Well, yes, but I've reconsidered. Rebecca had just as much motive. And she's the one who threw away the knife! Everyone's talking about the video. Why would she do that if she wasn't guilty?" Loretta accepted coffee from Lorraine, who'd begun preparing a cup as soon as Loretta entered. "Mark my words, it was Rebecca Crawford. You'll see."

After Loretta left—promising to return tomorrow with "more insights"—Lorraine collapsed dramatically into a chair.

"Mon Dieu, that woman! She is like a tornado of theories. First the mayor, then the judge, now the wife. Tomorrow she will probably suspect the dog!" Lorraine gestured at Mike, who wagged his tail innocently.

"She's certainly... enthusiastic," Emma said diplomatically.

"She's exhausting," Agatha corrected, but she was smiling. Despite everything—or perhaps because of it—Loretta's theatrical presence was almost entertaining. Like having a character from an Agatha Christie novel wander into real life.

But beneath the entertainment value, Agatha's detective instincts were noting certain facts. Loretta Thornton inherited Paul's estate. Not much, according to her, but enough to be a motive. She claimed to have been in Portland during the murder, but had she provided proof? Detective Dawson would verify, certainly, but still...

And her constant theories about everyone else—was that

genuine drama, or was it deflection? Keep pointing fingers at others so no one looked at you?

"Do you think she could have done it?" Emma asked quietly once Loretta was gone. "Killed her cousin for the inheritance?"

"She says she was in Portland," Agatha said. "But that's easy enough to claim."

"And she keeps changing her theories about who did it," Lorraine observed. "Always pointing at someone else. First this person, then that person. It is very suspicious, non?"

Agatha pulled out her notebook and made notes. Loretta Thornton—Paul's cousin and heir. Claims to have been in Portland. No apparent motive beyond inheritance. But the theatrical deflection, the constant accusations of others...

"I need to talk to Detective Dawson," Agatha said. "Find out if he's verified Loretta's alibi."

"You think she could have killed Paul?" Emma asked. "Her own cousin?"

"People have killed for less than an inheritance," Agatha said grimly. "And if Loretta's alibi doesn't hold up, she had means, motive, and opportunity."

"But the knife," Lorraine pointed out. "How would she have access to the Crawford knife?"

That was the question, wasn't it? The knife was the key to everything. Whoever killed Paul had taken that distinctive Norwegian silver blade from the Crawford house. Loretta would have had no access to their home, no way to steal it.

Unless...

"We need to find out if Loretta knew the Crawfords," Agatha said. "If she'd ever been to their house, maybe for some town event or function."

"She said she wasn't even in Bristol Lake," Emma reminded her.

"She said she was in Portland during the murder. That doesn't mean she was never in Bristol Lake before." Agatha tapped her pen against her notebook. "Someone took that knife. Someone who had access to the Crawford house. We need to know everyone who's been there."

As if summoned by the conversation, Agatha's phone buzzed with a text from Detective Dawson: *Loretta Thornton's alibi checks out. Was in Portland with friends during the tree lighting. Multiple witnesses confirm.*

Agatha showed the text to Emma and Lorraine.

"So she did not do it," Lorraine said, sounding almost disappointed.

"Or she has a very good alibi," Emma said. "Though I suppose multiple witnesses would be hard to fake."

Agatha studied the text, feeling frustrated. Another suspect cleared. Another dead end.

Loretta was dramatic, attention-seeking, and exhausting. But she wasn't a killer.

Which left them back where they'd started—with a shrinking pool of suspects and no clear answer.

"We're missing something," Agatha said for what felt like the hundredth time. "Something important."

Mike yawned and stretched, completely unconcerned with the mysteries of human behavior.

If only, Agatha thought, the truth was as simple as a dog's world—food, walks, and love.

But murder was never simple.

And this one was getting more complicated by the day.

Chapter 17

The Pattern Emerges

After Loretta's third dramatic exit, Agatha found herself thinking about something the woman had said: "Paul was such an important man. People relied on his expertise."

But people also feared that expertise, didn't they? Paul's thoroughness as a health inspector, his strict enforcement of regulations—these weren't just abstract qualities. They had real consequences for real people.

Emma must have been thinking along the same lines, because she looked up from her laptop at the café table and said, "We should look into Paul's work as a health inspector. Really look into it."

"Public records?" Agatha asked.

"Health inspection reports are public information. I can access them through the library's database." Emma's fingers were already flying over her keyboard. "If Paul was as thorough and strict as everyone says, there should be a trail of violations, citations, maybe even closures."

Lorraine appeared with fresh coffee for both of them.

"You are investigating Paul's work, oui? This is good. A man with power makes many enemies."

"Exactly," Agatha agreed. She pulled out her notebook, ready to take notes. "Emma, can you pull up Paul's inspection history for the past few years?"

"Already on it." Emma's screen filled with records. "Okay, Paul Chambers was a county health inspector for ten years. Started in 2014, worked continuously until... well, until last week. He was responsible for restaurants in Bristol Lake, Petunia Heights, Rockland, Oxford Hills, Camden, and several smaller towns."

"That's a lot of territory," Agatha observed.

"And a lot of restaurants." Emma scrolled through the data. "In the past five years alone, he conducted inspections at... let me count... over two hundred establishments."

"How many violations did he cite?" Lorraine leaned over Emma's shoulder, peering at the screen.

Emma clicked through several pages. "A lot. Way more than other inspectors in the county. Look at this—Inspector Rodriguez in the southern district cited violations at about thirty percent of the restaurants he inspected. Inspector Jones in the eastern district, about thirty-five percent. But Paul Chambers? Sixty-eight percent."

"That's double the rate," Agatha said, frowning.

"More than double. And look at the severity of the violations." Emma clicked on a specific report. "This restaurant in Oxford Hills—Paul cited them for twelve violations, including 'critical food safety risks.' But six months earlier, a different inspector had given them a clean report with only two minor issues noted."

"Perhaps they got worse in six months?" Lorraine suggested.

"Maybe. But look at this one." Emma pulled up another report. "Petunia Heights, a bakery. Paul shut them down for three days due to 'unsanitary conditions and evidence of pest infestation.' The owner filed a complaint, said the violations were exaggerated. A follow-up inspection by a different inspector found only minor issues and no evidence of pests."

Agatha's memory stirred. "Mike didn't like Paul. At the reception, remember? His ears went back, he wouldn't go near him. Mike's usually friendly with everyone."

"Your little detective dog knows bad people when he smells them," Lorraine said, patting Mike's head. The schnauzer had wandered over at the mention of his name, tail wagging hopefully for treats.

"Pull up the restaurants that closed after Paul's inspections," Agatha said. "Let's see how many there were."

Emma typed quickly, cross-referencing closure records with inspection reports. "In the past three years... seven restaurants closed within six months of receiving critical violations from Paul Chambers."

"Seven?" Agatha felt a chill. "That's a lot of failed businesses."

"And a lot of ruined lives," Emma added quietly. She clicked through the reports, reading aloud. "Villa Toscana in Petunia Heights—family-owned Italian restaurant, two generations. Closed after Paul cited them for fabricated health violations, according to the family's complaint. The Harborside Grill in Camden—cited for temperature violations and improper food storage. Closed three months later. Sullivan's Steakhouse in Rockland—"

"Wait," Agatha interrupted. "Pull up Villa Toscana again. What were the specific violations?"

Emma scrolled back. "Let's see... improper food temperature controls, evidence of cross-contamination, inadequate pest management, failure to maintain proper sanitation standards. It's a long list—fifteen violations total, eight of them critical."

"What happened after they closed?"

"According to this article from the Petunia Heights Gazette..." Emma clicked on a news link, "the owner, Anthony Greene, died six months after the restaurant closed. His widow claimed it was a broken heart. They'd owned the restaurant for twenty years, it was their entire livelihood."

"Mon Dieu," Lorraine breathed. "Paul destroyed them."

"Did any other restaurants contest Paul's findings?" Agatha asked.

"Several filed complaints with the county health department." Emma pulled up more records. "But most complaints were dismissed. Paul's reports were detailed, thorough, included photographs and documentation. The county backed him up every time. His record was impeccable—or so it seemed."

Agatha stood and began pacing, a habit when her mind was working through a puzzle. "Okay, so Paul was either extremely thorough and held restaurants to very high standards, or..."

"Or he was corrupt," Emma finished. "Using his position to shut down restaurants for reasons that had nothing to do with actual health violations."

"But why?" Lorraine asked. "What would he gain from closing restaurants?"

"Power," Agatha said slowly. "Control. Maybe money—if he was demanding payments to overlook violations, and restaurants that didn't pay got shut down."

"That's a serious accusation," Emma cautioned. "We don't have proof."

"No, we don't. But look at the pattern." Agatha gestured at the laptop screen. "Twice as many violations as other inspectors. Restaurants closing after his inspections. Complaints filed but dismissed. Multiple families claiming the violations were exaggerated or fabricated."

"Marina said Paul was very thorough,'" Emma remembered. "That he investigated everything, uncovered things people preferred to keep hidden. What if his thoroughness wasn't about public health? What if it was about finding leverage?"

AGATHA THOUGHT ABOUT THIS. Paul's reputation for thoroughness, for strict adherence to rules, for exposing secrets—it had made him respected in some circles. But it had also made him feared. And fear could be used as a weapon.

"We need to talk to these families," Agatha said. "The ones whose restaurants Paul closed. Find out what really happened."

"That's seven restaurants in three towns," Emma pointed out. "And some of those families might have moved away, started over somewhere else."

"Then we start with the ones we can find." Agatha pulled out her phone. "Lorraine, didn't you say you know someone in Petunia Heights? Someone who knows everyone's business?"

"Oui, my friend Beatrice! She is like me—she knows all the gossip, all the stories." Lorraine pulled out her own phone. "I will call her now, ask about these families."

While Lorraine stepped away to make her call, Agatha and Emma continued reviewing the inspection records. The pattern became clearer the more they looked. Paul's inspections were thorough, yes, but they were also unusually harsh. Minor infractions that other inspectors might overlook became critical violations in Paul's reports. Restaurants that received passing grades from other inspectors would fail Paul's inspection months later with dramatically different findings.

"Look at this," Emma said, pointing at her screen. "The Riverside Café in Bristol Lake. Inspector Chen gave them a passing grade in March. Paul inspected them in June and found ten violations. They closed in August."

"The Riverside Café?" Agatha remembered the place—a cheerful breakfast spot near the harbor, always busy on weekends. "They closed last summer. I didn't realize Paul was involved."

"According to this, he was the primary reason they closed." Emma read through the report. "The owner tried to contest the findings, said Paul was holding them to impossible standards. But the county sided with Paul."

Lorraine returned, her expression troubled. "Beatrice confirms what we suspected. Paul Chambers had a reputation in Petunia Heights—not a good one. She says several restaurant owners believed he was corrupt, that he demanded 'consulting fees' to overlook minor violations."

"Bribes," Agatha said flatly.

"BEATRICE DID NOT USE that word, but oui, essentially. She says it was whispered about but never proven. Paul was too careful, too smart." Lorraine sat down heavily. "And those who refused to pay? Their restaurants would fail inspection. Sometimes multiple times, until they had no choice but to close."

"How many families are we talking about?" Emma asked.

"In Petunia Heights alone? At least three in the past few years. And Beatrice says there were others in surrounding towns. Many others." Lorraine's dramatic flair was gone, replaced by genuine distress. "Paul destroyed lives, mes amies. Not just businesses—entire families."

Agatha felt the pieces of the puzzle shifting, forming a new picture. Not a murder motivated by personal grudges or old romantic history. A murder motivated by something much more primal: revenge for destroyed livelihoods, for lost dreams, for broken families.

"If Paul was corrupt, if he destroyed seven restaurants in three years..." Agatha calculated quickly, "that's at least seven families with strong motives to want him dead."

"Maybe more," Emma said. "These are just the ones that closed. What about restaurants that are still limping along after his inspections? Ones that paid his bribes but lost money doing it?"

"Or ones that survived but barely," Lorraine added. "Living under the threat that Paul could come back, inspect again, demand more money."

The scope of potential suspects had just expanded

dramatically. And somewhere in that pool of desperate, angry, ruined families, there might be a killer.

"We need to investigate these closed restaurants," Agatha said. "Talk to the families, find out who attended the tree lighting ceremony, who might have had access to the Crawford house."

"That's a lot of investigating," Emma said doubtfully. "We're talking about families across multiple towns. It could take weeks."

"Then we start with the closest ones," Agatha decided. "The Riverside Café here in Bristol Lake—the owner must still live in town. And Villa Toscana in Petunia Heights— that's only twenty miles away."

"I can research while you talk to people," Emma offered. "Pull up everything I can find about these restaurants, the families who owned them, what happened after they closed."

"AND I WILL TALK to my sources," Lorraine declared, her dramatic flair returning. "If Paul Chambers was corrupt, if he destroyed families for money, then everyone will want justice. I will find out everything people whispered but were too afraid to say out loud."

Agatha looked at her friends, feeling grateful for their support. This investigation had just taken a darker turn. Not a simple murder of a man with enemies, but potentially the execution of someone who'd wielded power like a weapon, who'd destroyed lives systematically, who'd hidden his corruption behind a veneer of thoroughness and professional standards.

If Paul Chambers was what they suspected—a corrupt

official who'd ruined families for personal gain—then his killer might not be a villain at all.

They might be someone seeking justice the only way they could find it.

But justice or revenge, murder was still murder.

And Agatha needed to find the truth.

"Tomorrow," she said, "we start talking to the families Paul destroyed. We find out who had the strongest motive, who had opportunity, who might have taken the Crawford knife to commit this murder."

Mike barked softly, as if agreeing with the plan.

"Your little detective approves," Lorraine said with a smile.

But Agatha wasn't smiling. Because somewhere in Bristol Lake or Petunia Heights or one of the surrounding towns, maybe there was a family whose life had been destroyed by Paul Chambers. A family desperate enough to kill.

Chapter 18

A Bitter Business

The drive to Rockland took thirty minutes through picturesque Maine countryside dusted with December snow. Agatha drove while Emma navigated and Lorraine provided running commentary on every Christmas decoration they passed. Mike sat in the back seat, nose pressed to the window, tail wagging at the prospect of adventure.

"Turn left at the next light," Emma said, consulting her phone. "The address is 42 Maple Avenue. According to my research, that's where the Sullivan family lives—they owned Sullivan's Steakhouse until it closed last year."

"Sullivan's," Lorraine mused from the back seat. "I remember that place! Such good food. The prime rib was magnifique."

"According to the inspection report, Paul cited them for temperature violations, improper storage, and cross-contamination risks," Emma read from her notes. "But previous inspections by other health officials showed only minor issues."

Agatha pulled up to a modest Cape Cod house with a cheerful wreath on the door and Christmas lights along the roofline. Despite the festive decorations, there was something tired about the property—peeling paint on the shutters, gutters that needed cleaning, a lawn that showed signs of deferred maintenance.

"Do we have a strategy?" Emma asked as they climbed out of the car. "We can't just knock on the door and ask if they murdered Paul Chambers."

"We'll say we're researching Paul's inspection practices for an article," Agatha suggested. "Or that we're concerned about fairness in the health inspection process."

"Or we could just tell the truth," Lorraine said cheerfully. "That Paul is dead, someone killed him, and we're trying to understand why."

"Lorraine!" Emma hissed.

"What? It is the truth, non?"

Before they could debate further, the front door opened. A woman in her sixties stepped out, wrapped in a cardigan despite the cold. "Can I help you? I saw you pull up."

"Mrs. Sullivan?" Agatha approached with her friendliest smile. "My name is Agatha Royale. I own One Deadly Chapter Books and Brew in Bristol Lake. I was hoping to ask you a few questions about Sullivan's Steakhouse. I understand it closed last year?"

The woman's expression immediately shuttered. "If you're from the health department—"

"We're not!" Emma said quickly. "We're just... trying to understand what happened to some of the restaurants Paul Chambers inspected."

At the mention of Paul's name, Mrs. Sullivan's face hardened. Then, surprisingly, she laughed—a bitter, tired sound. "You heard he's dead, then."

"Yes," Agatha said quietly.

"Good." Mrs. Sullivan crossed her arms. "I won't pretend to be sorry. That man destroyed my family's livelihood and never lost a moment of sleep over it." She studied them for a moment, then seemed to make a decision. "You might as well come in. It's too cold to stand out here talking."

The interior of the house was neat but worn, with furniture that had seen better days. Framed photographs on the walls showed happier times—the Sullivan family at what was clearly their restaurant, smiling in front of a large steakhouse sign, customers filling the dining room.

Mrs. Sullivan noticed Agatha looking at the photos. "That was five years ago, before Paul Chambers came into our lives. We had a good business. Twenty-three years we ran that steakhouse. It was packed every weekend, tourists and locals both. We were so proud."

She settled into an armchair, gesturing for them to sit on the couch. Mike immediately made himself comfortable at Agatha's feet.

"What happened?" Emma asked gently.

"Paul Chambers happened." Mrs. Sullivan's voice was matter-of-fact, but her hands trembled slightly. "He inspected our restaurant in March of last year. Found ten violations—temperature controls, storage procedures, food handling practices. Things we'd been doing the same way for twenty years with no problems. Every other inspector who'd come through gave us passing grades, maybe noted a minor issue here or there that we'd fix immediately."

"But Paul's inspection was different?" Agatha prompted.

"Paul's inspection was impossible. He held us to standards that no restaurant could meet. He took photographs of things that weren't even violations—a chef's apron with a small stain, a cutting board that showed normal wear, a thermometer that was off by half a degree." Mrs. Sullivan's voice rose slightly. "Half a degree! And he wrote it up like we were running a health hazard."

"Did you try to contest the findings?" Emma asked.

"Of course we did. Filed a formal complaint with the county health department. They sent another inspector three weeks later." Mrs. Sullivan gestured to a thick folder on the coffee table. "That inspector found two minor issues—a leaky faucet and a light bulb that needed replacing. Two minor issues! Not the ten critical violations Paul claimed."

"But by then the damage was done," Agatha guessed.

"By then, everyone in Rockland had seen the health department report posted in our window. 'Critical Violations —Reinspection Required.' People stopped coming. They'd say 'oh, we heard there were problems at Sullivan's' or 'isn't that the place that failed inspection?'" Mrs. Sullivan's eyes filled with tears. "We tried to rebuild our reputation, tried to explain that the violations were exaggerated. But once people think your food isn't safe, they don't come back."

"You closed six months later," Emma said, consulting her notes.

"Seven months. We fought as long as we could. Used our savings, took out loans, cut staff. But we couldn't recover from what Paul did to our reputation." Mrs. Sullivan wiped her eyes. "My husband had a heart attack three months after we closed. The stress, the financial worry, the loss of something we'd built our whole lives around. He's okay now, thank God, but we lost the business, lost our retirement savings, lost everything."

Lorraine made a sympathetic sound. "This is terrible. Simply terrible."

"We're not the only ones," Mrs. Sullivan continued. "I've talked to other restaurant owners Paul inspected. Some of them think he was corrupt—that he demanded money to overlook violations, and if you didn't pay, he'd shut you down."

"Did he demand money from you?" Agatha asked carefully.

Mrs. Sullivan hesitated. "Not directly. But about a week after that first inspection, he came back. Said he was there to 'consult' on bringing our restaurant up to standards. He suggested we hire him as a consultant—five thousand dollars to review our procedures and help us pass the next inspection. When I said we couldn't afford that, he got very cold. Said we'd better find a way to afford it if we wanted to stay in business."

"That's extortion," Emma breathed.

"That's Paul Chambers," Mrs. Sullivan corrected. "But we couldn't prove it. He never put anything in writing, never made explicit threats. He was too smart for that. And when we complained to the county, they said he was just offering professional advice, which wasn't against any rules."

"Did you hire him?" Agatha asked.

"We couldn't afford to. We used that money trying to fix the violations he'd cited, trying to meet his impossible standards." Mrs. Sullivan's voice was bitter. "And then he came back for the reinspection and found eight more violations.

Different ones this time. It was like he was determined to destroy us."

Mike whined softly, sensing the emotional tension in the room. Mrs. Sullivan looked down at him and managed a small smile.

"What a sweet dog. My husband always wanted a schnauzer." She reached down to pat Mike's head. "We were going to get one once the restaurant was stable, once we had more time. Now we can barely afford to feed ourselves, let alone a dog."

The simple statement broke Agatha's heart. This wasn't just about a business closure—it was about dreams deferred, lives derailed, futures stolen.

"Mrs. Sullivan," Agatha said gently, "were you at the Bristol Lake tree lighting ceremony last week?"

The woman looked up sharply. "Is that where Paul died?"

"Yes."

"Then no, I wasn't there. My husband and I don't go to town events anymore. We can't afford to, and frankly, we don't feel much like celebrating." Mrs. Sullivan's gaze sharpened. "But you're asking because you think whoever killed Paul might be someone he destroyed. Someone like us."

"We're trying to understand who had motive," Agatha admitted.

"Then you'll be talking to a lot of people," Mrs. Sullivan said. "Paul destroyed businesses all over this county. Some of them closed completely, like ours. Others survived but barely, living under the constant threat that Paul could come back, find more violations, demand more money. You want suspects? Go talk to the Greene family in Petunia Heights—

Villa Toscana. Or the Riverside Café in Bristol Lake. Or the bakery in Camden. There are dozens of families Paul hurt, and any one of them had reason to want him dead."

"But not you," Lorraine said. It wasn't quite a question.

"Not me," Mrs. Sullivan confirmed. "I'm not sorry he's dead—I won't pretend to be. But I didn't kill him. My husband and I were home that night, watching television, trying to forget that we used to be successful business owners and are now struggling to pay our mortgage."

The bitterness in her voice was painful to hear. After a few more questions—none of which yielded useful information—Agatha, Emma, and Lorraine thanked Mrs. Sullivan and left.

Back in the car, Lorraine let out a heavy sigh. "That poor woman. Paul truly was a monster, non?"

"He destroyed her life," Emma agreed quietly. "And she's just one of many."

Agatha started the car, her mind working through what they'd learned. Mrs. Sullivan had motive—strong motive. But she also had no connection to the Crawford house, no way to obtain the knife. And her alibi, while uncorroborated, seemed genuine. Two people at home watching television weren't likely to have committed murder at a crowded town square twenty miles away.

"Where to next?" Emma asked.

"The Riverside Café in Bristol Lake," Agatha decided. "If we're going to talk to Paul's victims, we might as well start with the ones closest to home."

～

THE RIVERSIDE CAFÉ had been a beloved breakfast spot, perched near the harbor with views of the water. Now it sat empty, a "For Lease" sign in the window, the cheerful blue awning faded and torn.

Emma checked her notes. "The owners were Martha and David Murphy. According to my research, they still live in Bristol Lake—just moved to a smaller place after the restaurant closed."

They found the Murphys in a modest apartment above the hardware store on Central Avenue. Martha answered the door with a baby on her hip and a toddler clinging to her leg.

"Yes?" She looked harried, exhausted in the way of young mothers managing small children alone.

"Mrs. Murphy? I'm Agatha Royale. I own One Deadly Chapter Books and Brew. I was hoping to ask about the Riverside Café."

Martha's expression immediately turned wary. "I don't want to talk about that. It's in the past."

"Please," Emma said. "It's about Paul Chambers."

"I heard he died." Martha shifted the baby to her other hip. "I'm sorry that happened, but I really don't want to discuss it. I have enough problems without dredging up old ones."

"Did Paul demand money from you?" Agatha asked directly. "For consulting fees or to overlook violations?"

Martha's eyes widened. Then, abruptly, she laughed—a sound somewhere between amusement and despair. "Oh, you've talked to others, then. Yes, Paul wanted money. Three thousand dollars to 'help us meet health standards.' When we refused, suddenly we had critical violations that appeared out of nowhere. Our business died within three months."

"We're so sorry," Lorraine said sympathetically. "You have such beautiful children. This must be very difficult."

"Difficult doesn't begin to cover it," Martha said tiredly. "My husband works two jobs now. I take care of the kids and do online bookkeeping from home. We're barely making it. And all because Paul Chambers decided we wouldn't pay his bribe."

"Were you at the tree lighting ceremony?" Agatha asked.

"God, no. We couldn't afford a babysitter, and we're too exhausted to take the kids to crowded events." Martha's baby began to fuss, and she bounced him automatically. "Look, I need to get dinner started. Was there anything else?"

There wasn't, really. Another family destroyed by Paul's corruption, another potential suspect with strong motive but no apparent opportunity.

BY THE TIME they returned to Bristol Lake, the winter sun was setting. They'd visited four families in total—the Sullivans in Rockland, the Murphys in Bristol Lake, a bakery owner in Camden, and a café owner in Oxford Hills. Every story was similar: Paul's excessive violations, his demands for money, businesses closing or struggling, families devastated.

"This is so depressing," Emma said as they pulled up to One Deadly Chapter. "How many lives did Paul destroy?"

"Too many," Agatha said grimly. "And any one of these families could have killed him. The question is—did one of them?"

"They all have motive," Lorraine observed. "Strong motive."

"But do they have opportunity?" Emma asked. "None of them mentioned knowing the Crawfords or being at their house. How would they get the knife?"

Agatha stared out at the darkening street, frustration gnawing at her. "I don't know. Maybe one of them found a way. Maybe one of them was at a town event at the Crawford house and stole the knife then. Or maybe..."

"Maybe what?" Emma prompted.

"Maybe we're looking at this wrong," Agatha said slowly. "Maybe the knife isn't the key. Maybe Dennis or Rebecca really did kill Paul, and all this corruption we've uncovered is just context—motive on top of motive."

"You don't believe that," Lorraine said.

"I don't know what I believe anymore." Agatha rubbed her temples. "The evidence against the Crawfords is overwhelming. But these families Paul destroyed—they had just as much reason to want him dead. More, even. The Crawfords lost an engagement twenty years ago. These people lost their entire livelihoods, their futures, their dreams."

"So what do we do?" Emma asked.

"We keep digging," Agatha said. "We find out if any of these families had connections to Bristol Lake, to the Crawfords, to that ceremony. We look for opportunity to go with motive."

"And if we don't find it?"

"Then maybe the obvious answer is the right one," Agatha said quietly. "Maybe Dennis or Rebecca did kill Paul, and we've been chasing shadows."

Chapter 19

Expanding the Investigation

Emma called Agatha early the next morning, her voice excited. "I found something. Or rather, someone."

"Tell me," Agatha said, cradling her phone against her shoulder as she poured coffee for herself and filled Mike's water bowl.

"Thomas Barrett. He owned The Harbor Grille in Winthrop—about fifteen miles from Bristol Lake. Paul shut him down eighteen months ago." Emma's voice rose with excitement. "But here's the interesting part—Thomas Barrett attended the tree lighting ceremony. I found his name on the sign-in sheet for parking."

Agatha's pulse quickened. "He was there?"

"He was there. And get this—when I looked him up on social media, he made several posts about Paul over the past year. Angry posts. One from three months ago said 'Paul Chambers will get what's coming to him. Karma always wins.'"

"That sounds like a threat."

"It gets better. The Harbor Grille was a family business—Thomas's father started it forty years ago, Thomas took it over fifteen years ago. It was their legacy, their pride. And Paul destroyed it over what Thomas claimed were fabricated violations." Emma paused dramatically. "Thomas lost everything. Had to move his family into his parents' house. His wife left him six months ago, took the kids. He's been working construction to make ends meet."

"So he has motive," Agatha said slowly. "And he was at the ceremony. That's opportunity."

"Exactly. I think we need to talk to him."

"Does Detective Dawson know about this?"

"Not yet," Emma said. "I mean, attending a public ceremony and posting angry things on social media isn't really evidence of murder. I thought we should talk to Thomas first, see if there's anything more concrete before we bother Dawson with it."

"Good thinking," Agatha agreed. "If Thomas has a solid alibi or a good explanation, there's no point involving the police. But if he seems like a real suspect..."

"Then we take what we learn to Dawson," Emma finished. "Though Agatha, be careful. If Thomas really did kill Paul, he could be dangerous."

An hour later, Agatha and Emma drove to Winthrop with Mike in the back seat. Lorraine had wanted to come, but Agatha thought three people might be too intimidating. Better to keep it casual, friendly, non-threatening.

The address Emma had found led them to a weathered cape house on the outskirts of Winthrop. The yard was overgrown, Christmas decorations from years past hung broken from the eaves, and a rusted truck sat in the driveway.

"Not exactly prosperity," Emma murmured as they climbed out of the car.

A man in his forties answered their knock. Thomas Barrett was tall and broad-shouldered, with the kind of build that came from physical labor. His face was weathered, angry lines etched deep around his mouth and eyes. When he saw them, his expression immediately turned suspicious.

"If you're selling something, I'm not interested."

"Mr. Barrett? I'm Agatha Royale, and this is Emma Fletcher. We're not selling anything. We wanted to talk to you about The Harbor Grille."

His face darkened. "I have nothing to say about that place."

"We're investigating Paul Chambers's death," Agatha said carefully. "We know he inspected your restaurant. We know what happened."

"Good." Thomas's voice was harsh. "I hope whoever killed him sleeps well at night. That bastard deserved what he got."

The naked hostility was startling. Emma took a small step back, but Agatha held her ground.

"Can we come in? Just for a few minutes?"

Thomas studied them for a long moment, then shrugged. "Why not? Not like I have anything to hide."

The interior of the house was sparse—minimal furniture, boxes stacked against walls suggesting he'd never fully unpacked, dishes piled in the sink. Through a doorway, Agatha could see an older couple sitting in front of a television—Thomas's parents, presumably.

"My folks," Thomas said, noticing her glance. "I moved

back here after I lost everything. Forty-two years old and living with my parents like I'm a kid again."

"I'm sorry," Emma said quietly.

"Don't be sorry. Be angry. Paul Chambers destroyed my life for no reason except I wouldn't pay his extortion money." Thomas gestured for them to sit on a worn couch. "You know about the bribes?"

"We've heard from other restaurant owners," Agatha confirmed. "That Paul demanded consulting fees."

"Five thousand dollars. That's what he wanted from me. Five grand to overlook the violations he'd invented." Thomas's hands clenched into fists. "I told him to go to hell. The Harbor Grille had been in my family for forty years. We'd passed every inspection, had an spotless reputation. I wasn't going to let some corrupt inspector shake me down."

"What happened after you refused?" Emma asked.

"He came back two weeks later with a list of critical violations. Improper temperature controls, cross-contamination risks, evidence of rodent activity—all lies. Complete fabrications." Thomas's voice rose. "I demanded a reinspection by a different official. They found nothing. But by then, the damage was done. Word got out that The Harbor Grille had failed inspection, and people stopped coming."

"You closed?"

"Six months later. Used every penny of savings trying to stay afloat. Took out loans. Borrowed from my parents, from friends. Nothing worked." Thomas stood abruptly, pacing. "My wife couldn't take the stress. Said I was obsessed with revenge against Paul, that I needed to let it go and move on. When I wouldn't, she left. Took my kids. I haven't seen them in three months."

The raw pain in his voice was genuine. Agatha felt sympathy despite the anger radiating from him.

"Mr. Barrett," she said gently, "we understand you were at the Bristol Lake tree lighting ceremony last week."

Thomas stopped pacing. His expression shifted—guarded, wary. "So what if I was?"

"Can you tell us why you attended? Bristol Lake is fifteen miles from here."

"I like Christmas displays. Is that a crime?"

"No, but—"

"But you want to know if I killed Paul." Thomas laughed, a bitter sound. "Everyone's probably thinking it, right? Angry guy whose life Paul destroyed, shows up at the ceremony where Paul dies. Must be guilty."

"We're just trying to understand what happened," Emma said carefully.

"What happened is that Paul Chambers finally got what he deserved." Thomas sat down heavily. "I was there. I saw him at the ceremony, saw him judging another town's Christmas display like he had any right to judge anything. And I thought about how many lives he'd destroyed, how many families he'd ruined. I thought about my kids, about my wife, about everything I'd lost because that man decided I wouldn't pay his bribe."

"What did you do?" Agatha asked quietly.

"Nothing. I stood there in the crowd, watched the tree light up, and fantasized about telling Paul exactly what I thought of him. About making him understand what he'd done to me, to my family." Thomas's voice dropped. "But I didn't do anything. I just stood there like a coward and watched him walk away."

"Where were you during the tree lighting? Between 7:15 and 7:30?"

Thomas's expression shuttered. "In the crowd. Watching the ceremony like everyone else."

"Can anyone verify that? Did you stand with anyone, talk to anyone during those minutes?"

"No. I was alone." His jaw tightened. "Is that what you came here for? To accuse me of murder?"

"We're not accusing anyone," Agatha said. "We're trying to find the truth."

"The truth is that Paul Chambers destroyed my life, and I'm not sorry he's dead. If that makes me a suspect, fine. But I didn't kill him." Thomas stood, clearly done with the conversation. "I thought about it. God knows I thought about it. But I didn't do it."

"Mr. Barrett—" Emma began.

"I think you should leave now." Thomas walked to the door and opened it. "I've told you everything I'm going to tell you. If the police want to question me, they can. But I'm done talking."

They had no choice but to leave. Back in the car, Emma let out a shaky breath.

"He's angry enough to kill," she said. "And he was there, at the ceremony, with no alibi."

"He's also in pain," Agatha said, starting the engine. "Angry, desperate, destroyed. But does that make him a killer?"

"He has motive, opportunity, and he openly admits he fantasized about confronting Paul." Emma checked her notes. "Agatha, this could be our guy."

Mike whined from the back seat, and Agatha glanced at

him in the rearview mirror. The schnauzer looked uneasy, his ears slightly back—the way he got around people who made him nervous.

"Detective Dawson needs to know about this," Agatha said. "Thomas Barrett needs to be questioned officially."

"Do you think he did it?" Emma asked.

Agatha thought about Thomas's anger, his bitterness, his admission that he'd fantasized about confronting Paul. She thought about his lack of alibi, his presence at the ceremony, his openly stated hatred of the victim.

"I think he's our strongest suspect yet," she admitted. "But something feels... I don't know. Off."

"Off how?"

"If Thomas killed Paul, where did he get the Crawford knife? How would he have access to their house?" Agatha tapped her fingers on the steering wheel. "That's the piece that doesn't fit."

"Maybe he didn't use the Crawford knife," Emma suggested. "Maybe he brought his own knife, and someone else disposed of the Crawford knife separately. Two unrelated events that just happened to occur at the same time."

It was possible. Unlikely, but possible.

"We need to find out if Thomas Barrett has any connection to the Crawfords," Agatha said. "Any reason he would have been in their house, any way he could have taken that knife."

"And if he doesn't?"

"Then either he's innocent, or he's very clever." Agatha pulled onto the main road. "Either way, Detective Dawson needs to investigate him thoroughly."

She called Dawson from the car, relaying everything

Thomas had said. The detective listened carefully, asked a few questions, then was quiet for a moment.

"Interesting," Dawson said finally. "Barrett was at the ceremony, he has strong motive, and he's openly hostile about Paul's death. But attending a public event and being angry isn't enough for formal questioning."

"What are you going to do?" Agatha asked.

"I'll verify what you've told me - check if he was really at the ceremony, look into his social media posts, see if there's any connection between Barrett and the Crawford house. If what you're telling me checks out and I can find anything more concrete, then I'll bring him in for formal questioning." Dawson paused. "Good work, Agatha. This is the strongest lead we've had. If Barrett can't provide a solid alibi and we can connect him to the Crawford knife somehow, we might have our killer."

After hanging up, Agatha and Emma drove back to Bristol Lake in thoughtful silence. The winter landscape passed by—snow-covered fields, decorated houses, the occasional Christmas tree visible through windows.

"Do you think we solved it?" Emma finally asked. "Is Thomas Barrett the killer?"

"Maybe," Agatha said. But doubt nagged at her. "Or maybe he's exactly what he appears to be—a destroyed man who hated Paul Chambers but didn't kill him."

"Then who did?"

That was the question. If not Thomas Barrett, with his obvious motive and presence at the ceremony, then who?

The Crawford knife was still the key. Someone had taken it, used it, disposed of it. Until they found out who had access to that knife, they couldn't solve this case.

"We need that list from Dennis," Agatha said. "The cleaning service employees. That's our next step."

"You really think someone from the cleaning service did it?"

"I think someone who had access to the Crawford house did it. And the cleaning service is the most logical connection." Agatha pulled into her parking spot behind One Deadly Chapter. "Tomorrow, I'll press Dennis for that list."

Mike barked from the back seat, eager to get out and stretch his legs.

As they climbed out of the car, Emma said quietly, "Thomas Barrett looked guilty, Agatha. Really guilty."

"I know," Agatha agreed. "But looking guilty and being guilty aren't always the same thing."

Though as she unlocked the bookstore and let Mike inside, she couldn't shake the image of Thomas's face—the anger, the bitterness, the open admission that he'd fantasized about confronting Paul.

If Thomas Barrett wasn't the killer, he was certainly a convincing suspect.

And maybe that was all the real killer needed—someone else to take the blame.

Chapter 20

The False Lead

Detective Dawson called Agatha the next afternoon. She answered on the second ring, hopeful for news.

"Thomas Barrett's alibi checked out," Dawson said without preamble. "He's cleared."

Agatha's heart sank. "What? How?"

"I brought him in this morning for formal questioning. He was cooperative, if angry. Maintained he didn't kill Paul, that he just attended the ceremony." Dawson paused. "Then I verified his timeline. Turns out he wasn't alone at the ceremony after all."

"He told us he was alone," Emma said—she'd been restocking shelves nearby and hurried over when she heard Dawson's name.

"He was alone when he arrived, but around 7:15—right before the tree lighting—he ran into three friends from Winthrop. They were at the ceremony together, and they stood together watching the tree light up. All three confirm

Thomas was with them from 7:15 until well after 8:00, when news of the body spread through the crowd."

Agatha felt frustration wash over her. "He could have asked them to lie for him."

"I considered that. But one of the friends showed me photos from the ceremony—timestamped photos that clearly show Thomas in the background at 7:22 and 7:28. He's visible in the crowd, far from where Paul's body was found. There's no way he could have committed the murder during that window." Dawson's tone was matter-of-fact. "Barrett had motive, he was at the scene, and he openly hated Paul. But he didn't kill him."

After hanging up, Agatha slumped into one of the café chairs. Mike immediately came over, resting his chin on her knee.

"Another dead end," Emma said, sitting across from her. "Thomas seemed so guilty."

"He seemed angry," Agatha corrected. "And he is angry— he has every right to be after what Paul did to him. But angry doesn't equal guilty."

Lorraine swept in from the back room where she'd been organizing book club materials. "What is this long face I see? Did something happen?"

"Thomas Barrett has an alibi," Emma explained. "He's been cleared."

"Ah." Lorraine settled into a chair. "So we are back to the beginning, non?"

Not quite the beginning, Agatha thought. They'd learned a great deal—about Paul's corruption, about the families he'd destroyed, about the breadth of people who had motive to kill him. But none of that brought them closer to identifying the actual killer.

"How many suspects have we cleared now?" Emma pulled out her notebook, flipping through pages. "Patricia Anderson—solid alibi, was in the bathroom line. Robert Coleman—at Eliza's bakery buying cookies. Marina Hawkins —with her boyfriend on the bench near Maple Street. Loretta Thornton—in Portland with friends. And now Thomas Barrett—with friends in the crowd."

"And yet the Crawfords, who everyone suspects, we don't actually think did it," Lorraine added. "Even though all the evidence points to them."

"Because the evidence is too convenient," Agatha said. But even as she spoke, doubt crept in. Was it too convenient? Or was she overthinking this? Maybe Dennis or Rebecca really had killed Paul in a moment of rage, using a knife from their own home without thinking about the consequences.

"What about the other families?" Emma asked. "The ones whose restaurants Paul closed? Should we investigate all of them?"

"That could be dozens of people," Agatha said wearily. "And we've already talked to several. The Sullivans in Rockland were home watching television. The Murphys in Bristol Lake couldn't afford a babysitter. The bakery owner in Camden was visiting family in Portland. Everyone either has an alibi or wasn't at the ceremony."

"So we have dozens of suspects with motive," Emma summarized, "but no one with both motive and opportunity. Except the Crawfords."

The words hung in the air, heavy with implication.

Mike whined and pressed closer to Agatha's leg. She

scratched behind his ears absently, her mind working through the puzzle that refused to come together.

"The knife," she said suddenly. "We keep coming back to the knife. Someone took it from the Crawford house. That's the key we're missing."

"Dennis said many people have been in their house," Lorraine reminded her. "Town council meetings, Ladies' Guild gatherings, contractors, the cleaning service. It could be anyone."

"Then we need to narrow it down," Agatha said, feeling a spark of determination. "We need that list of everyone who's had access to the Crawford house in the past two months. And we need to cross-reference it with people who had motives to kill Paul."

"Dennis said he'd get you the cleaning service list," Emma said. "Have you followed up on that?"

Agatha pulled out her phone. "I'll text him now."

She sent a quick message: *Dennis, following up on that cleaning service employee list. Can you send it today?*

The response came quickly: *Will get it from Rebecca and send by tonight. She handles all the household scheduling.*

"He's sending it tonight," Agatha reported.

"And then what?" Lorraine asked. "We investigate every person who cleans the Crawford house?"

"If we have to, yes." Agatha stood, pacing the bookstore floor—a habit when her mind was working through problems. "Whoever killed Paul had to have access to that knife. It's the one concrete fact we have. So we find out who had access, cross-reference with who had motive, and see if any names overlap."

"That's a lot of work," Emma said doubtfully.

"Then we'd better get started." Agatha pulled out her notebook, opening to a fresh page. "Emma, can you compile a master list of all the families Paul hurt? Everyone whose restaurant closed, everyone who filed complaints against him, everyone we've identified as potential victims of his corruption?"

"I can do that," Emma said, already pulling out her laptop.

"And I," Lorraine declared, "will continue to gather gossip. If there are connections between these families and Bristol Lake, my sources will know."

They worked through the afternoon, building lists, researching connections, trying to find the thread that would tie everything together. The bookstore had a few customers, but Celeste—Agatha's part-time assistant—was working and handled them while Agatha focused on the investigation.

Around four o'clock, Celeste brought them coffee and cookies from Eliza's bakery. "You all look very serious," she observed. "Still investigating the murder?"

"Trying to," Agatha said. "Though we seem to keep hitting dead ends."

"Well, if anyone can solve it, you can," Celeste said with confidence. "You've solved every other mystery in Bristol Lake."

After she left, Emma looked up from her laptop. "Okay, I have a preliminary list. Seventeen families whose restaurants were closed or severely damaged by Paul's inspections in the past three years. That's not counting restaurants that survived but had to pay his bribes."

"Seventeen," Agatha repeated. "That's a lot of potential suspects."

"And that's just the restaurants we know about," Emma added. "There could be others that closed quietly, or that moved away and didn't file complaints."

Lorraine had been making phone calls, working her network of gossips and informants. "I have learned something interesting, mes amies. Three of the families on Emma's list have connections to Bristol Lake."

"Which three?" Agatha asked, leaning forward.

"The Sullivan family from Rockland—the wife's sister lives in Bristol Lake and works at the pharmacy. The Martinez family from Oxford Hills—they have cousins who own the antique shop on Central Avenue. And..." Lorraine paused dramatically, "the Greene family from Petunia Heights. The mother, Catherine Greene, works as a house cleaner. And one of her regular clients is a family in Bristol Lake."

Agatha's pulse quickened. "Which family?"

"Lorraine's source didn't know," Lorraine admitted. "But a house cleaner would have access to homes, non? Access to dining rooms, kitchens, places where valuable items are kept?"

"Like a cabinet displaying Norwegian silver," Emma breathed.

"It's a connection," Agatha said carefully. "But we need to verify it. Dennis is sending the cleaning service list tonight. If Catherine Greene's name is on it, if she cleans the Crawford house, then we have a real lead."

"And if she's not on the list?" Emma asked.

"Then we keep looking." But Agatha felt a flutter of hope. Catherine Greene—a woman whose family restaurant had been destroyed by Paul, whose husband had died from the stress, who worked as a house cleaner and might have had access to the Crawford house.

It was tenuous, but it was something.

"We wait for Dennis's list," Agatha decided. "And then we start investigating every name on it, looking for connections to Paul's victims."

The afternoon faded into evening. Customers came and went. Agatha tried to focus on normal bookstore operations, but her mind kept returning to the case. Seventeen families. Dozens of potential suspects. And somewhere in that tangle of destroyed lives and desperate people was a killer.

Her phone buzzed with a text from Dennis: *Cleaning service list attached. Hope it helps.*

Agatha opened the attachment with trembling fingers. The list showed names, dates, and which areas of the house each person had cleaned over the past two months.

She scanned through the names, looking for Catherine Greene.

Her heart sank. The name wasn't there.

"She's not on the list," Agatha said, disappointment heavy in her voice.

Emma looked over her shoulder. "Are you sure? Maybe she uses a different name, or—"

"I checked. Catherine Greene, Cathy Greene, C. Greene —none of them appear." Agatha set her phone down. "Another dead end."

Lorraine peered at the list. "But there are other names, non? Other people who could have taken the knife?"

There were. Twelve different employees had cleaned the Crawford house over the past two months. Twelve names to investigate, to cross-reference with Paul's victims, to somehow connect to the murder.

"Tomorrow," Agatha said tiredly. "Tomorrow we start going through these names, finding out who they are, whether any of them had connections to Paul or reasons to want him dead."

"It's a lot of work," Emma said gently.

"It's all we have." Agatha closed her notebook. "Somewhere in this mess of suspects and motives and opportunities is the truth. We just have to find it."

But as she locked up the bookstore that evening and headed home with Mike, Agatha couldn't shake the feeling that they were missing something. Something important, hiding in plain sight.

Thomas Barrett had seemed so guilty. His anger, his presence at the ceremony, his open hatred of Paul—all of it had pointed to him as the killer.

But he wasn't. He was just another victim of Paul's corruption, another person destroyed by a man who wielded power like a weapon.

The real killer was still out there, watching the investigation stumble from one dead end to another, probably feeling very safe.

Chapter 21

Lorraine's Discovery

Agatha was halfway through shelving a new shipment of mysteries when Lorraine burst through the bookstore door with all the drama of a stage actress making an entrance. Her purple coat billowed behind her, her scarf trailed dramatically, and her eyes gleamed with the thrill of discovery.

"Agatha! Emma! I have found something!" She swept across the bookstore floor, nearly colliding with a startled customer browsing the Christie section. "Pardonnez-moi! But this is urgent!"

Mike lifted his head from his spot by the fireplace, assessed that Lorraine wasn't bringing treats, and settled back down with a contented sigh.

"Lorraine," Agatha said, setting down the books she'd been holding, "what's happened?"

"I have been investigating!" Lorraine announced, loud enough that the few customers in the store glanced over curiously. "Talking to everyone, asking questions, being—how do you say—discreet."

Emma, who'd been helping a customer at the register, finished the transaction and hurried over. "What did you find out?"

Lorraine pulled off her coat with a flourish and draped it over a chair, then settled into the café area as if preparing for a grand performance. "You know I have been talking to people about the Crawfords, oui? Trying to understand who they are, who knows them, who has been to their house."

"Yes," Agatha said patiently, joining her at the table. "And?"

"And I have discovered something very interesting!" Lorraine paused for dramatic effect. "The Crawfords have a cleaning service. A woman comes to their house twice a week to clean."

Agatha blinked. "We already knew that. Dennis mentioned it when we talked to him."

"Ah, but did you know that this cleaning woman sees everything in their house?" Lorraine leaned forward conspiratorially. "She dusts the cabinets, she organizes the dining room, she has access to every room. Including where the knife was kept!"

"That's... actually a good point," Emma said slowly. "A cleaning person would have had access to the knife cabinet."

"Exactement!" Lorraine beamed. "So I thought, perhaps this cleaning woman saw something? Perhaps she knows who took the knife? Or perhaps..." Lorraine's eyes widened dramatically, "perhaps she took it herself!"

"Why would a cleaning woman take the knife?" Agatha asked, though she was making notes in her ever-present notebook. "What would be her motive?"

"I do not know! But she has access, non? And in mysteries, the person with access is always suspicious." Lorraine sat back, clearly pleased with herself. "I have done detective work, just like you!"

"You have," Agatha agreed with a smile. "And it's good information. Thank you, Lorraine."

"So we will investigate this cleaning woman?"

Agatha glanced at the list Dennis had sent—the twelve names of cleaning service employees who'd worked at the Crawford house. "We'll look into it. But right now, I'm more focused on the families Paul destroyed. They had much stronger motives than a random cleaning person."

"But motive without opportunity is nothing," Lorraine insisted. "And this cleaning woman has opportunity!"

"She does," Emma agreed. "But Lorraine, we'd need to connect her to Paul somehow. Find a reason she'd want him dead."

"Perhaps she is related to one of the families whose restaurants closed?" Lorraine suggested. "Perhaps Paul destroyed her brother's business, or her sister's café, and she sought revenge?"

"It's possible," Agatha said, though she didn't sound convinced. Her mind was still on Thomas Barrett and the other obvious suspects—people with clear, strong motives who'd lost everything because of Paul's corruption.

"I will continue investigating," Lorraine declared. "I will find out everything about this cleaning service and the people who work there."

"That would be helpful," Agatha said, meaning it. Even if the cleaning service angle seemed like a long shot, it was still worth exploring. "In the meantime, Emma and I are going through the list of restaurant families, trying to find connections."

"Pah!" Lorraine waved this away. "You are looking in the wrong place, mes amies. The answer is closer than you think —it is always so in mystery novels. The butler, the maid, the person who has access but no one suspects!"

"Life isn't always like mystery novels," Emma said gently.

"Is it not?" Lorraine's expression turned knowing. "We shall see."

A customer approached with a question about a book recommendation, and Agatha excused herself to help. By the time she returned, Lorraine had moved on to a different theory entirely.

"Or perhaps," Lorraine was saying to Emma, "it was one of the other judges! Patricia Anderson seemed very stern, very controlled. What if she was hiding a secret passion for Paul, and when he rejected her, she killed him in jealous rage?"

"Patricia has a solid alibi," Emma reminded her. "She was in the bathroom line with witnesses."

"Alibis can be faked!" Lorraine insisted. "In mysteries, the person with the perfect alibi is always the killer."

"I thought you just said the person with access but no one suspects is always the killer," Emma pointed out, trying not to smile.

"It can be both! Mystery is full of surprises, non?"

Over the next hour, as Agatha worked and customers came and went, Lorraine offered a steady stream of theories. Perhaps it was Rebecca after all, driven mad by seeing her former fiancé. Perhaps it was Dennis in a crime of passion. Perhaps it was the mayor's secretary, secretly embezzling

funds and Paul had discovered it. Perhaps it was Gladys—"
She is always so sweet, but the sweetest ones are often hiding
darkness, I have read this in many books!"

Each theory was more elaborate than the last, and each
was gently dismissed by Agatha and Emma. But through it
all, Lorraine kept circling back to the cleaning service.

"You must investigate these cleaning people," she
insisted. "Mark my words, the answer lies there!"

"We'll look into it," Agatha promised, though her attention remained on the restaurant families. Those were the
people with real motive, real reason to want Paul dead. A
cleaning person seemed too random, too disconnected from
Paul's crimes.

Finally, Lorraine gathered her coat and scarf, preparing
to leave. "I will continue my research," she announced. "And
when I solve this mystery before you do, I will be very
gracious about it!"

After she left, Emma collapsed into a chair with a laugh.
"She means well."

"She does," Agatha agreed, smiling despite her frustration with the case. "And who knows? Maybe she's right about
the cleaning service. It's worth checking out."

"After we finish with the restaurant families," Emma
said.

"After we finish with the restaurant families," Agatha
confirmed.

But as she returned to shelving books, Lorraine's words
echoed in her mind: "The person with access but no one
suspects."

The cleaning service had access to the Crawford house,
to the dining room, to the cabinet where the knife was kept.

But without motive, without any connection to Paul, what reason would any of them have to commit murder?

Unless...

Unless one of them was connected to the restaurant families. Unless one of the cleaning people had a relative or friend whose business Paul had destroyed. Then they'd have both motive and opportunity.

Agatha pulled out the list Dennis had sent, studying the twelve names again. Tomorrow, she'd start researching each one, looking for connections to Paul's victims.

It was probably a long shot. The real killer was likely one of the restaurant owners themselves, or a family member, or someone with a direct grudge against Paul.

But Lorraine had planted a seed of doubt. And in Agatha's experience, seeds of doubt often grew into important revelations.

"Emma," she called out, "can you help me research these cleaning service employees? See if any of them have connections to the families on our list?"

"Of course." Emma came over, pulling out her laptop. "Though it might take a while. That's twelve people to investigate."

"Then we'd better start now."

They worked through the afternoon, searching social media, public records, any information they could find about the twelve cleaning service employees. Most were exactly what they appeared to be—working people trying to make a living, with no apparent connection to Paul Chambers or his victims.

But three names stood out. Three people whose backgrounds needed deeper investigation.

One had a sister who'd worked at a restaurant Paul had shut down.

One had lived in Petunia Heights before moving to Bristol Lake.

And one—Catherine Greene—had owned a restaurant that Paul had destroyed.

Agatha's pulse quickened as she read Catherine Greene's sparse social media profile. Worked as a house cleaner. Former restaurant owner. Lived in Petunia Heights.

"Emma, look at this."

Emma leaned over, scanning the information. "Catherine Greene. Isn't that—"

"Villa Toscana," Agatha said. "The Italian restaurant in Petunia Heights. The one Mrs. Sullivan mentioned, the one that closed after Paul's inspection."

"But she's not on the Crawford cleaning service list," Emma pointed out. "We already checked."

"We checked for Catherine Greene specifically," Agatha said slowly. "But what if she works for the cleaning service under a different name? A married name, or a maiden name, or—"

Her phone rang, interrupting the thought. Detective Dawson.

"Agatha, wanted to update you. Thomas Barrett's alibi is solid. I've cleared him as a suspect."

They'd already known this, but hearing it confirmed still felt like a setback. "So we're back to square one."

"Not quite. I've been looking into the cleaning service angle you mentioned. The list Dennis sent you—I ran background checks on all twelve employees."

"And?"

"Most are clean. No connections to Paul or his victims that I can find. But there's one name I want to dig into deeper. Catherine Greene. She owned a restaurant Paul shut down, and she works for the cleaning service that covers several homes in Bristol Lake."

Agatha's heart raced. "Does she clean the Crawford house?"

"That's what I'm trying to verify. The cleaning service is being cagey about giving me specific client assignments without a warrant, and I don't have enough for a warrant yet. But I'm working on it."

After hanging up, Agatha stared at her notebook where she'd written Catherine Greene's name and circled it twice.

A woman whose restaurant was destroyed by Paul. A woman who worked as a house cleaner. A woman who might have had access to the Crawford house and the Norwegian silver knife.

But it was still just speculation. Without proof that Catherine had cleaned the Crawford house, without evidence connecting her to the murder, it was just another theory in a case full of dead ends.

"We need to keep investigating the restaurant families," Agatha said firmly. "Thomas Barrett was a dead end, but there are still others. People with motive who were at the ceremony."

"And Catherine Greene?" Emma asked.

"We keep her name on the list. But we don't jump to conclusions." Agatha closed her notebook. "Lorraine might be right that the cleaning service is important. But we need evidence, not just theories."

Chapter 22

Dawson's Frustration

Detective Dawson arrived at One Deadly Chapter just after noon, looking more tired than Agatha had ever seen him. He accepted the coffee she offered with a grateful nod and settled into one of the café chairs with a heavy sigh.

"That bad?" Agatha asked, sitting across from him with her own cup. Mike immediately positioned himself between them, hoping for attention from both directions.

"We've been working this case for over a week," Dawson said, scratching Mike's ears absently. "I've interviewed dozens of people, followed up on every lead, and I feel like I'm running in circles."

Emma emerged from the back room with a plate of Eliza's Christmas cookies—gingerbread snowmen with cheerful icing smiles. "You both look like you need these," she said, setting them on the table.

"Bless you," Dawson said, taking two. "I've been living on coffee and vending machine sandwiches. Real food is a nice change."

"How many suspects have we investigated now?" Agatha asked, pulling out her notebook. "I've lost count."

"Too many." Dawson pulled out his own notes. "The judges—all cleared with solid alibis. Loretta Thornton—in Portland with witnesses. Thomas Barrett—seemed perfect until his alibi checked out. Multiple restaurant owners whose lives Paul destroyed—all either have alibis or weren't at the ceremony."

"And yet someone killed Paul," Emma said, joining them with her laptop. "Someone who was there, who had access to the Crawford knife, who planned it carefully enough to commit murder in front of two hundred witnesses."

"That's what keeps bothering me," Dawson said, running a hand through his hair. "This wasn't a crime of passion. Whoever did this brought the Crawford knife specifically, used it during the exact window when everyone was distracted by the tree lighting, and disappeared back into the crowd. That's planning. That's calculation."

"But throwing the knife in a trash bin suggests panic," Agatha pointed out. "Those two things don't fit together."

"Unless different people were involved," Dawson suggested. "One person committed the murder, another disposed of the weapon. Which brings us back to—"

"The Crawfords," Agatha finished quietly.

They sat in silence for a moment, the only sound Mike's contented panting as Emma scratched behind his ears.

"I don't want it to be them," Dawson admitted. "Dennis Crawford is the mayor, for God's sake. Rebecca is a pillar of the community. But Agatha, the evidence..."

"I know." Agatha stared into her coffee. "Their knife,

their motive, Dennis finding the body and lying about it, Rebecca disposing of the weapon. It all points to them."

"And their stories don't match," Dawson added. "Dennis claims Rebecca told him the knife was already gone when she checked. But the video clearly shows her throwing it away. Someone's lying."

"They're protecting each other," Emma said. "That much is obvious."

"But from what?" Agatha asked. "From a murder charge? Or from something else?"

Dawson ate another cookie, chewing thoughtfully. "Sometimes in my line of work, you reach a point where you have to accept the obvious answer. Not everything is a clever mystery with a twist ending. Sometimes the person who looks guilty is guilty."

"You think one of them did it," Agatha said.

"I think it's the most logical explanation for all the evidence." Dawson spread his hands helplessly. "Dennis and Rebecca had twenty years of resentment toward Paul. They had access to the knife—it was in their own house. They were both at the ceremony with no solid alibis. Dennis found the body and fled without reporting it. Rebecca disposed of the murder weapon. What am I supposed to think?"

"That someone very clever framed them," Agatha said, but even she could hear the doubt in her voice.

"Who?" Dawson challenged gently. "Who had access to their knife? Who knew about their history with Paul? Who could have planned this so perfectly?"

Agatha opened her mouth to answer, then closed it. She didn't have an answer. Every suspect they'd investigated had been cleared or couldn't be connected to the Crawford house.

Except Catherine Greene, a small voice in her head whispered. The cleaning woman whose restaurant Paul destroyed.

But even that was speculation. They had no proof Catherine had ever cleaned the Crawford house, no evidence she'd taken the knife, nothing but Lorraine's dramatic theories and Agatha's desperate hope that the Crawfords were innocent.

"I don't know," Agatha admitted finally. "I don't know who framed them. But something feels wrong about Dennis or Rebecca being killers."

"Feelings aren't evidence," Dawson said, though not unkindly. "I wish they were. Would make my job easier."

Lorraine swept in from outside, bringing a gust of cold December air and her usual dramatic energy. "Ah, Detective Dawson! You are here! I have been thinking about the case, and I have a new theory—"

"Lorraine," Agatha interrupted gently, "maybe now isn't the best time."

But Dawson smiled tiredly. "Actually, I could use a good theory right now, even if it's far-fetched. What have you got, Mrs. Dubois?"

Lorraine settled into a chair, clearly delighted to have an audience. "I have been thinking about the cleaning service, as I mentioned to Agatha. And I believe the killer must be someone who worked in the Crawford house. Someone who saw the knife, recognized its value, and decided to use it to frame them!"

"That's... actually not a bad theory," Dawson said.

"We've been looking into the cleaning service employees. Most are dead ends, but there's one—Catherine Greene—who owned a restaurant Paul shut down. Problem is, I can't verify if she actually cleaned the Crawford house. The service won't release client assignments without a warrant, and I don't have probable cause for a warrant."

"Why not?" Emma asked.

"Because owning a failed restaurant and working as a cleaner doesn't equal murder," Dawson explained. "I need more—proof she had access to the Crawford house, evidence she was at the tree lighting, something concrete that connects her to the crime."

"And you don't have it," Agatha said.

"Not yet." Dawson finished his coffee. "Meanwhile, the prosecutor is breathing down my neck about Rebecca Crawford. He thinks we have enough to charge her with obstruction at minimum, possibly conspiracy to commit murder. Dennis too."

"When?" Agatha asked, alarm rising.

"Soon. Maybe as early as tomorrow." Dawson stood, looking reluctant. "I'm sorry, Agatha. I know you wanted a different answer. But unless we find solid evidence pointing to someone else, the Crawfords are going to face charges."

After he left, the three of them sat in gloomy silence. Even Mike seemed to sense the mood, resting his chin on Agatha's foot with a sympathetic whine.

"We've been investigating for over a week," Emma said quietly. "And we're no closer to the truth than when we started."

"We know Paul was corrupt," Agatha countered. "We

know he destroyed families. We know there are dozens of people who wanted him dead."

"But we can't connect any of them to the murder," Emma finished. "Motive without opportunity is useless."

Lorraine, unusually subdued, sipped her coffee. "Perhaps Detective Dawson is right. Perhaps sometimes the obvious answer is the correct one, even in mysteries."

"You don't believe that," Agatha said. "You're the one who keeps insisting it's never the obvious suspect."

"I am also the one who watches too many television shows and reads too many novels," Lorraine admitted. "Perhaps real life is more boring than fiction, non?"

Agatha looked at her notebook, at the pages filled with names and theories and dead ends. They'd worked so hard, investigated so thoroughly, and yet they kept coming back to the same conclusion: Dennis and Rebecca Crawford looked guilty.

Maybe they were guilty. Maybe Agatha's instincts were wrong this time.

But something still nagged at her. The knife in the trash bin. The planning versus the panic. The way the evidence was almost too perfect.

"We have until tomorrow," she said finally. "One more day before Rebecca gets arrested. If we're going to find the real killer, we need to do it now."

"How?" Emma asked. "We've run out of leads."

"Then we go back to what we know," Agatha said, forcing determination into her voice. "Catherine Greene worked for a cleaning service. Lorraine, can you find out which service and get a list of their clients?"

"I can try," Lorraine said, perking up. "My cousin's

daughter works for a cleaning company. Perhaps she knows something."

"Emma, keep researching Catherine Greene. Find out everything you can about her—where she lives, if she has family in Bristol Lake, anything that might connect her to the Crawfords or the ceremony."

"On it," Emma said, opening her laptop.

"And what will you do?" Lorraine asked.

"I'm going to talk to Celeste," Agatha said. "She's from Petunia Heights. Maybe she knows the Greene family, or Villa Toscana, or something that can help us."

It was a long shot. Everything at this point was a long shot.

But Agatha had learned over the years that sometimes the smallest details—the things everyone overlooked because they seemed insignificant—were the keys that unlocked entire mysteries.

They had one day. Twenty-four hours before Rebecca Crawford faced arrest and the case closed with the wrong person charged.

One day to find the truth.

Mike barked softly, as if offering encouragement, and Agatha reached down to pat his head.

"We can do this," she said, trying to convince herself as much as her friends. "We've solved cases before. We can solve this one."

"Before tomorrow?" Emma asked doubtfully.

"I don't know," Agatha admitted. "But we're going to try."

Chapter 23

The Holiday Continues

Despite everything—the murder, the investigation, the looming arrest of Rebecca Crawford—Christmas was still coming to Bristol Lake. Agatha discovered this fact anew each morning when she opened the bookstore to find customers eager for holiday shopping, their arms full of gift lists and their faces bright with seasonal cheer.

"Do you have any Agatha Christie first editions?" a woman asked, browsing the Christie Corner with careful attention. "My mother collects them."

"I have a few," Agatha said, pulling out her catalog. "Let me show you what's available."

Mike dozed by the fireplace, a small Santa hat perched rakishly on his head—Emma's doing. He'd tolerated the indignity for approximately thirty seconds before shaking it off, but Emma kept replacing it, and eventually Mike seemed to accept his fate as a festive schnauzer.

The bookstore looked beautiful, Agatha had to admit.

Garlands draped the shelves, white lights twinkled through-out, and a small tree in the café corner was decorated with book-themed ornaments. Eliza had sent over trays of Christmas cookies—gingerbread, sugar cookies shaped like books, peppermint bark. The scent of cinnamon and pine filled the air.

It should have felt magical. Instead, Agatha felt the weight of time running out. Tomorrow, Rebecca Crawford would likely be arrested. And they were no closer to finding the real killer.

"Agatha?" Celeste appeared at her elbow, her long braided hair decorated with a festive red ribbon. "The woman in the cozy mystery section wants recommendations for her book club. Can you help her?"

"Of course." Agatha pushed her worries aside and summoned her best bookstore owner smile.

The afternoon passed in a blur of customers and ques-tions. A grandfather looking for mysteries for his teenage granddaughter. A young woman buying books for her mother. A retired couple wanting recommendations for their winter reading. Everyone seemed determined to find the perfect books, to make Christmas special despite the shadow of murder hanging over the town.

"People are still talking about it," Emma murmured during a brief lull, gesturing to two women whispering near the true crime section. "I've heard at least five different theo-ries today about who killed Paul."

"Let me guess," Agatha said tiredly. "The Crawfords?"

"Mostly. Though Mrs. Henderson is convinced it was someone from out of town—a professional hit man hired by one of the restaurant owners." Emma tried not to smile. "She watches too many crime shows."

"Don't we all," Agatha muttered.

Lorraine swept in around three o'clock, her purple coat dusted with fresh snow. "It is snowing again! Très beautiful!" She stamped her boots on the mat and pulled off her gloves. "Any news, mes amies?"

"Nothing yet," Agatha admitted. "You?"

"My cousin's daughter confirmed that Catherine Greene works for Spotless Home Cleaning Service. But she does not know which houses Catherine cleans—that information is confidential." Lorraine's disappointment was evident. "Without a warrant, we cannot force them to tell us."

"So we're stuck," Emma said.

"For now," Agatha said, refusing to give up hope. "But there has to be another way to find out if Catherine cleaned the Crawford house."

The bell above the door chimed, and another customer entered—a woman in her early twenties with a warm smile and an armful of shopping bags. She had dark hair pulled back in a ponytail and wore a cheerful red scarf that matched her mittens.

"Oh my gosh, Larissa!" Celeste looked up from restocking shelves, her face brightening. "I haven't seen you in forever!"

"Celeste! Hi!" The young woman set down her bags and gave Celeste a quick hug. "I'm doing some last-minute Christmas shopping. Thought I'd stop by—I heard about this place from friends. It looks amazing!"

"Isn't it great?" Celeste beamed with pride, as if she

owned the store herself. "I work here part-time. Best job ever."

Agatha, helping another customer select gift wrap at the register, glanced over briefly and smiled. It was nice to see Celeste connecting with someone her own age. The girl worked hard and deserved to enjoy herself.

"Are you home for the holidays?" Celeste asked.

"Just for a few days. I've been working in Portland, but I always come back for Christmas." Larissa browsed the nearest shelf, pulling out a cozy mystery. "My mom loves these. She's been reading more lately—says it helps her relax after work."

"Oh, she'll love that one," Celeste said enthusiastically. "The whole series is really good. Very Agatha Christie-esque."

"Perfect. I'll take it." Larissa collected a few more books, chatting easily with Celeste about mutual friends, changes in Petunia Heights, plans for Christmas. Her laugh was light and genuine, her manner friendly and warm.

Agatha barely registered the conversation, too focused on wrapping books and processing sales. The afternoon rush had begun—people getting off work, stopping by to browse, desperate to finish their Christmas shopping before the big day.

"This is for my mom," Larissa said when she reached the register, setting down four mysteries and a coffee table book about Maine lighthouses. "She deserves something nice. She works so hard."

"I'm sure she'll love them," Agatha said, scanning the books and sliding them into a bag. "Would you like gift wrap?"

"Yes, please. Thank you so much." Larissa handed over her credit card with a smile. "This place is wonderful. I'll have to come back more often."

"We'd love that," Agatha said warmly, processing the payment. "Have a lovely Christmas."

"You too!" Larissa collected her bags and waved to Celeste. "See you around!"

"Bye!" Celeste called out, then returned to shelving books.

Agatha turned to help the next customer—an elderly man looking for a specific Dorothy Sayers novel—her mind already moving on to the next transaction.

Agatha turned to help the next customer—an elderly man looking for a specific Dorothy Sayers novel—and forgot about Larissa almost immediately.

The afternoon wore on. More customers, more sales, more cheerful conversations about books and Christmas plans. Someone asked about the murder—"terrible thing, during such a beautiful ceremony"—and Agatha gave her standard response: the police were investigating, justice would prevail, Bristol Lake remained a safe community.

Around five o'clock, the crowd finally thinned. Emma collapsed into a café chair with a dramatic sigh. "I love the holiday rush, but my feet are killing me."

"Mine too," Celeste agreed, joining her. "At least we made good sales. Agatha, the register totals look great."

"Small blessing," Agatha said, though she appreciated it. The bookstore was doing well despite—or perhaps because of—the recent tragedy. People seemed to crave the comfort of books, the escape into fictional mysteries with tidy solutions.

If only real mysteries were so neat.

"That was nice, seeing your friend," Emma said to Celeste. "Larissa, was it?"

"Oh yeah! We went to high school together in Petunia Heights. She was a couple years ahead of me, but we had theater class together." Celeste stretched her arms over her head. "She's really nice. I'm glad she's doing well—she had a rough time for a while."

"Oh?" Emma asked, her natural curiosity piqued.

But before Celeste could elaborate, another customer entered with a question about special ordering a book, and the conversation shifted.

The evening passed quietly. A few more customers trickled in, but the rush was over. Lorraine left to make dinner. Emma worked on restocking shelves. Celeste organized the café area.

And Agatha stood at the window, looking out at Central Avenue with its Christmas lights and decorated storefronts, thinking about what the morning would bring.

Rebecca Crawford would likely be arrested. The case would effectively close with the wrong person charged, and a killer would walk free.

Unless Agatha could find proof—real, concrete proof—that someone else had committed the crime.

"We're missing something," she said quietly, more to herself than anyone else.

Mike came over and pressed against her leg, offering silent support. She reached down to scratch his ears, drawing comfort from his steady presence.

"Closing time," Emma announced, checking her watch. "Want me to lock up?"

"Please." Agatha continued staring out the window, her mind churning through facts and theories and dead ends.

The snow was falling harder now, coating Bristol Lake in fresh white. The Christmas tree in the town square still glowed, still beautiful, still a reminder of the celebration that had turned deadly.

"Before tomorrow?" Emma asked doubtfully.

"I don't know," Agatha admitted. "But we're going to try."

Chapter 24

Rebecca's Arrest

Agatha was arranging a display of Christmas mysteries in the front window when Emma burst through the door, her cheeks flushed from the cold.

"They arrested Rebecca," Emma said breathlessly. "About an hour ago. It's all over town."

Agatha set down the books she'd been holding. "Dawson said it was coming."

"I know, but still. Seeing her being led into the police station..." Emma shook her head. "Half the town was there. Mrs. Henderson said Rebecca looked calm, composed even. Like she'd been expecting it."

"She probably was," Agatha said, moving behind the register to check the morning sales. "The evidence against her has been mounting for days."

Lorraine arrived moments later, also full of news. "Rebecca Crawford has been arrested! Can you believe it? The mayor's wife, charged with murder!"

"We heard," Emma said.

"What are the charges exactly?" Agatha asked, pulling out her notebook.

"Murder and obstruction of justice," Lorraine reported, clearly having gathered all the details. "The prosecutor says she disposed of the murder weapon, had strong motive, and no alibi for the time of the killing."

"What about Dennis?" Emma asked.

"Not charged yet, but still under investigation. They think he might have been involved too, or at least helped cover it up." Lorraine settled into a café chair. "The whole town is talking about nothing else."

Mike wandered over from his spot by the fireplace, sensing the energy in the room. Agatha reached down to pet him, organizing her thoughts.

"Do you think she did it?" Emma asked quietly. "Really did it?"

"I don't know," Agatha admitted. And that was the truth. She'd been so focused on investigating other suspects, so certain the Crawfords were being framed, but maybe she'd been wrong. Maybe Rebecca really had killed Paul in a moment of rage and panic. "The evidence is pretty damning."

"But your instincts—" Lorraine began.

"My instincts have been wrong before," Agatha interrupted gently. "And Detective Dawson is right—sometimes the obvious answer is the correct one. Rebecca disposed of the murder weapon. That's not speculation, that's video evidence."

"So that's it?" Emma asked. "Case closed?"

"Maybe." Agatha flipped through her notebook,

reviewing all their dead-end investigations. "Or maybe we're still missing something."

The bell above the door chimed, and several customers entered, chattering excitedly about the arrest. Agatha put on her professional smile and helped them find books, but her mind kept working through the puzzle.

If Rebecca killed Paul, where was the planning? The calculation? Using her own family knife, disposing of it in a public trash bin—those were acts of panic, not premeditation. But luring Paul behind the tree stand during a crowded ceremony required planning.

The two things still didn't fit together properly.

Around noon, Detective Dawson stopped by, looking tired but not unhappy.

"You heard," he said, accepting the coffee Agatha offered.

"The whole town heard," Agatha said. "How's Rebecca?"

"Maintaining her innocence. Says she didn't kill Paul, that she was 'protecting someone.'" Dawson sipped his coffee. "She won't elaborate on who or what she was protecting them from."

"Dennis?" Emma suggested.

"That's the assumption. That she thinks Dennis killed Paul and she's covering for him. Or vice versa—Dennis thinks Rebecca did it and he's protecting her." Dawson shrugged. "Either way, one or both of them are involved. The prosecutor is confident we have enough for a conviction."

"What about the other suspects?" Agatha asked. "The restaurant families, Catherine Greene, all the people Paul destroyed?"

"The case is closed, Agatha. We have our suspect in

custody." Dawson set down his cup. "I know you wanted a different answer. You were convinced someone framed the Crawfords. But the evidence speaks for itself—Rebecca disposed of the murder weapon. That's not something an innocent person does."

"What if she found it and panicked—"

"Then she should have called the police immediately." Dawson's tone was gentle but firm. "Look, I understand you want to believe the best of people. But sometimes the obvious answer really is the correct one. Rebecca Crawford is facing charges, and unless something dramatic changes, she'll likely be convicted."

After he left, Agatha stood at the window, watching the lunchtime shoppers hurry past with their bags and packages. Christmas was three days away. The town square's tree still glowed each evening. Life in Bristol Lake continued despite murder and arrest and broken trust.

"What do we do now?" Emma asked.

"I don't know," Agatha admitted. "Keep the bookstore running. Finish Christmas shopping. Maybe accept that we did our best but couldn't solve this one."

"You're giving up?" Lorraine sounded shocked.

"I'm accepting reality," Agatha corrected. "Rebecca is in custody. The prosecutor thinks he has enough evidence. Maybe he's right."

But even as she said it, something nagged at her. That familiar feeling when puzzle pieces didn't quite fit, when the picture wasn't complete.

The afternoon passed normally enough. Customers came and went. Celeste arrived for her shift, full of sympathy for the Crawfords. "It's so sad," she said. "Rebecca always seemed so nice."

"Seemed," Agatha noted. "Past tense."

"Well, I mean... if she really did it..." Celeste trailed off uncomfortably.

The day wound down. Sales were good—people still wanted books for Christmas. The bookstore felt warm and welcoming despite the cold December evening outside.

Agatha was preparing to close when her phone buzzed with a text from Dawson: *Rebecca's arraignment tomorrow at 10am. Bail will likely be granted—she's not a flight risk. But trial will proceed.*

So that was that. The case was moving forward, with or without definitive proof.

"Are you okay?" Emma asked as they locked up.

"I'm fine," Agatha said. "Just... thinking."

"About the case?"

"About whether we missed something important. Or whether there was nothing to miss." Agatha pulled on her coat. "Maybe Rebecca really is guilty, and I've been chasing shadows."

"Or maybe the real killer is out there, watching Rebecca take the fall," Emma said quietly.

That was the question, wasn't it?

Agatha drove home through the snowy evening, Mike asleep in the passenger seat. The Christmas lights along the streets blurred together, cheerful and bright against the dark December sky.

Tomorrow, Rebecca's arraignment. Then the slow march toward trial. Then conviction, probably, given the evidence.

Unless something changed. Unless some new information came to light.

But Agatha had run out of leads to follow, suspects to investigate, theories to pursue.

She'd done her best.

Sometimes, that had to be enough.

Even when it didn't feel like enough at all.

Chapter 25

The Celebration

Rebecca Crawford's arraignment was brief and, according to Emma who'd attended, surprisingly undramatic. The judge granted bail—Rebecca was a prominent community member with deep roots in Bristol Lake and no flight risk. She'd return home to Dennis and await trial.

"She looked tired," Emma reported when she returned to the bookstore around noon, "but composed. Dennis was there, of course. He held her hand the whole time."

"At least they have each other," Agatha said, arranging a display of last-minute gift books. Two days until Christmas, and people were still shopping frantically.

"Mon Dieu, what a relief!" Lorraine swept through the door with her usual dramatic flair, unwinding her purple scarf with a flourish. "Rebecca is home! I saw her and Dennis at the pharmacy just now. She was buying—what do you call it—headache medicine. Poor thing looked exhausted, but she smiled at everyone. Such grace under pressure!"

"Did you talk to her?" Emma asked.

"Mais non! What would I say? 'Hello, alleged murderess, lovely weather we're having?'" Lorraine helped herself to a gingerbread cookie from the tray on the café table. "Though I wanted to. Lorraine Dubois is dying of curiosity, but she has restraint. Sometimes."

Agatha smiled despite herself. "Your restraint is admirable."

"It is a burden I bear," Lorraine said dramatically, taking a bite of cookie. "Oh! These are magnifique! Eliza has outdone herself. You know, if I ever committed murder—which I would not, of course—I would do it for Eliza's cookies. They are worth dying for. Or killing for. Perhaps both!"

"Lorraine!" Emma laughed.

"What? I am French! We are passionate about food!" Lorraine looked around as if someone might contradict her, then settled into a chair with a satisfied nod, pulling Mike onto her lap. The schnauzer accepted the attention with his usual good nature. "But seriously, mes amies, do you think Rebecca really killed Paul? Now that she has been arrested, charged, released on bail—it seems so real, non?"

"It is real," Agatha said. "Whether she's guilty or not, she's facing trial."

"But you still have doubts, oui? I can see it in your face." Lorraine fed Mike a small piece of cookie, which he accepted graciously. "You think someone else did it."

"I think..." Agatha paused, choosing her words carefully. "I think the evidence points to Rebecca. But I can't quite make all the pieces fit together."

"Then we keep investigating!" Lorraine declared. "Until the trial, there is still time!"

"To investigate what?" Emma asked reasonably. "We've

run out of leads, Lorraine. Every suspect we've looked into either has an alibi or no connection to the Crawford knife."

"Then we look harder! We ask more questions! We—oh!" Lorraine's attention was diverted by the bell above the door. "A customer! Perhaps she needs a book recommendation. Lorraine knows all the best mysteries!"

The customer was Larissa, the young woman from Petunia Heights who'd been in a few days ago. She smiled when she saw Celeste restocking shelves near the register.

"Hi again!" Larissa said cheerfully. "I'm back for more books. My mom loved what I got her last time."

"Oh, that's wonderful!" Celeste beamed. "What's she interested in now?"

"Anything cozy and Christmasy. She's been reading a lot lately—says it helps her relax after work." Larissa browsed the holiday mystery display Agatha had just finished arranging. "These look perfect."

Agatha came over to help. "Looking for anything specific?"

"Just something light and fun. My mom's had a tough year, and I want her Christmas to be nice." Larissa's smile was warm and genuine. "She works so hard—long hours, you know. But she never complains."

"Your mother sounds wonderful," Agatha said.

"She is. She's the best." Larissa selected three Christmas mysteries and a cozy mystery cookbook. "These should do it. Oh, and maybe some of those gingerbread cookies? They smell amazing."

"From Eliza's Cottage Bakery," Lorraine chimed in, having drifted over with her natural nosiness. "The best in Bristol Lake! You have excellent taste, mademoiselle."

"Thank you!" Larissa laughed. "I'm Larissa, by the way. I'm from Petunia Heights, but I love coming to Bristol Lake. It's so charming here."

"Larissa and I went to high school together," Celeste explained to Agatha. "She's visiting for the holidays."

"Well, we're glad you're here," Agatha said, ringing up the books. "Did you enjoy the tree lighting ceremony last week? I know what happened was terrible, but the tree was beautiful."

"Oh, it was gorgeous!" Larissa's enthusiasm seemed genuine. "Such a special event. I'm so glad I got to see it, even though..." She trailed off delicately.

"Even though someone was murdered," Lorraine finished with her typical lack of filter. "Très tragique! But at least they caught who did it, non?"

"I heard about the arrest," Larissa said. "It's good that justice is being served. That poor man—Paul Chambers—he deserved better."

Something about the way she said it struck Agatha as odd, but before she could think about it, another customer called for help finding a specific book.

"Excuse me," Agatha said, handing Larissa her bag. "Merry Christmas!"

"Merry Christmas to you too!" Larissa waved to Celeste. "See you around!"

After she left, Lorraine munched thoughtfully on another cookie. "Such a nice girl. Very polite. Good taste in books." She paused dramatically. "Though I wonder..."

"Wonder what?" Emma asked.

"Nothing! Just Lorraine being suspicious of everyone, as usual." Lorraine laughed at herself. "After investigating for weeks, I see murderers everywhere! Perhaps that nice girl who buys books for her maman is secretly a criminal master-mind! Perhaps Mike is the killer!" She gestured at the schnauzer, who wagged his tail. "Look how innocent he pretends to be!"

"You've definitely been reading too many mysteries," Emma said, laughing.

The afternoon passed pleasantly. More customers, more sales, more cheerful holiday conversations. The weight of the investigation seemed to lift slightly—Rebecca was home on bail, the prosecutor was confident in his case, and life in Bristol Lake was returning to something like normal.

Even if normal included a murder trial on the horizon.

Around four o'clock, Gladys stopped by with a sugges-tion. "Agatha, dear, are we still having book club after Christ-mas? I think we could all use the normalcy."

"Of course," Agatha said. "I was thinking we'd discuss the latest Louise Penny?"

"Excellent. Though I do hope," Gladys said with a knowing look, "that we'll stick to fictional mysteries this time. We've had quite enough of the real thing."

"Wise decision," Agatha agreed.

"Though I must say," Gladys continued, selecting a book from the new releases, "I'm surprised it was Rebecca. I always thought Dennis was the more likely suspect, tempera-mentally speaking."

"Perhaps they were in it together!" Lorraine suggested dramatically. "Like Bonnie and Clyde! Or—what is the French couple—Bonnie et Clyde!"

"That's the same couple, Lorraine," Emma pointed out.

"Exactement! They are famous in any language!"

After Gladys left, Lorraine helped close up the bookstore, chattering the entire time about various murder theories, Christmas plans, and whether Mike needed a new sweater.

"He has his natural coat, Lorraine," Agatha reminded her. "Yes, but a festive sweater! With reindeer!"

As Agatha locked the door and prepared to head home, she felt oddly content. They hadn't solved the case the way she'd hoped. Rebecca was facing charges she might not deserve. But Bristol Lake was still beautiful, Christmas was still coming, and her bookstore was thriving.

Sometimes, she supposed, that had to be enough.

"À demain!" Lorraine called out, pulling on her gloves and wrapping her purple scarf more tightly. "Tomorrow we will have more adventures! Perhaps solve more crimes! Or at least eat more cookies!"

Agatha smiled and waved, then locked the door and headed toward Knob Hill with Mike trotting beside her, his breath forming little puffs in the cold air.

The investigation was effectively over. Rebecca would face trial, probably be convicted, and life would move on.

It should have felt like closure.

Instead, it felt like something left undone.

But what? What was she missing?

Mike trotted contentedly beside her, completely unconcerned with unsolved mysteries.

Maybe she should follow his example, Agatha thought. Accept that some cases didn't have neat endings, some puzzles didn't get solved.

Maybe Rebecca really was guilty, and that was simply the truth of it.

The walk home felt longer than usual, the December

cold seeping through her coat. She tried to quiet the voice in her head that whispered: *something's wrong, something doesn't fit, you're missing something important.*

But what?

What was she missing?

Chapter 26

Celeste's Comment

The next morning, the bookstore was quiet—the calm after the holiday shopping storm. Christmas Eve was tomorrow, and most people were home wrapping presents and preparing for family celebrations.

Celeste arrived for her shift around ten, bundling in from the cold with snowflakes dusting her braided hair.

"Quiet day?" she asked, unwinding her scarf.

"Very," Agatha said. She was inventorying stock, checking what had sold during the rush and what needed reordering for the new year. Mike dozed by the fireplace, enjoying the peaceful morning.

Emma was at the library—she'd texted that morning saying she had some last-minute research to finish before the holiday closure. Lorraine hadn't appeared yet, probably sleeping in after days of dramatic investigating.

Celeste made herself coffee and settled at the café table with her laptop. "I have an essay due next week," she explained. "Thought I'd work on it during the slow period. Hope that's okay?"

"Of course," Agatha said. "Take advantage of the quiet while you can."

They worked companionably for an hour—Celeste typing, Agatha organizing shelves, Mike occasionally sighing in his sleep. The bookstore felt cozy and warm, insulated from the December cold outside.

Around eleven, Celeste stretched and looked up from her laptop. "That was nice seeing Larissa yesterday. I hadn't seen her in months."

"She seemed lovely," Agatha said, dusting a shelf of classic mysteries. "Very thoughtful, buying all those books for her mother."

"She's always been like that. So caring." Celeste sighed, a sad sound. "Poor girl. I always felt sorry for her."

Something in Celeste's tone made Agatha pause. "Sorry for her? Why?"

"Oh, you know. Everything that happened with her family." Celeste took a sip of coffee. "When their restaurant closed. It was so awful."

Agatha's hands stilled on the books. "What restaurant?"

"Villa Toscana. In Petunia Heights." Celeste's expression was sympathetic. "It was this beautiful Italian place—the Greene family ran it. Larissa's grandfather started it, then her father took over. Best food you've ever had. My parents used to take me there for special occasions."

Villa Toscana. The name rang a bell. Agatha had seen it in Emma's research—one of the restaurants Paul Chambers had shut down.

"The Greene family?" Agatha asked carefully.

"Yeah, Larissa Greene. Her dad was Anthony Greene— everyone loved him. Nicest guy, always remembered your name, gave kids free cannoli." Celeste smiled at the memory, then her expression sobered. "But then—"

The door burst open with a cheerful jingle of bells, and a woman in her sixties swept in, humming "Jingle Bells" loudly. She wore a bright red coat with jingle bell earrings that tinkled with every movement.

"Hello, hello!" she sang out, her voice carrying the melody. "Dashing through the snow, in a one-horse open sleigh—oh, good morning! What a beautiful bookstore! I'm visiting my daughter for Christmas and she said I simply must stop by One Deadly Chapter. What a clever name!"

Agatha smiled and moved to help her. "Welcome! Are you looking for anything specific?"

"Mystery novels! I adore them. The cozier the better. Nothing too dark or violent—I get enough of that on the news." The woman's jingle bell earrings chimed as she examined the shelves. "Oh, these look perfect! And look at this adorable dog! What's his name?"

"Mike," Agatha said as the woman bent to pet him. Mike, ever sociable, wagged his tail and accepted the attention graciously.

"Such a sweet boy! My daughter won't let me have a dog —says I travel too much. But I do miss having one." The woman straightened, her bells tinkling. "Now, which of these would you recommend? I want something festive for reading by the fire tomorrow."

Agatha spent ten minutes helping her select books, wrapping them in festive paper, and listening to stories about the woman's daughter, her grandchildren, and her plans for Christmas dinner. The whole interaction was delightfully normal, a bright spot of holiday cheer.

"Merry Christmas!" the woman called out as she left, bells jingling. She actually did a little dance step on the sidewalk outside, still humming "Jingle Bells."

"She was fun," Celeste said with a laugh.

"Very festive," Agatha agreed, smiling. But as she returned to the café table, her mind shifted back to their earlier conversation. "You were telling me about Villa Toscana. The Greene family restaurant?"

"Oh, right." Celeste's cheerful expression faded. "It was really sad what happened. The health department shut them down—said they had all these violations. But everyone knew it was garbage. That place was spotless. My parents swore the inspector made it all up."

Agatha's heartbeat quickened. "Do you remember which inspector?"

"Paul Chambers." Celeste said the name with obvious distaste. "Everyone in Petunia Heights knows his name. He shut down like three or four restaurants over the years. People hated him."

Paul Chambers. The murdered man. The corrupt inspector who'd destroyed families for money.

"What happened to the Greene family after the restaurant closed?" Agatha asked, trying to keep her voice casual.

"It destroyed them," Celeste said simply. "Mr. Greene—Larissa's dad—he tried to fight it, filed complaints, but the county sided with the inspector. They lost everything. The restaurant was their whole life, you know? Three generations of work, just gone."

"That's terrible," Agatha said quietly.

"It got worse. Mr. Greene died about six months later. Heart attack, officially, but everyone said it was a broken heart. He couldn't handle losing the restaurant." Celeste's eyes were sad. "Larissa had to drop out of college to help support the family. She'd been studying at UMaine, wanted to be a teacher. Had to leave, get a job. And her mom—Mrs. Greene—she had to find work. It's been really hard on them."

Catherine Greene. The name that had come up in their investigation. The woman who worked for a cleaning service.

"Does Mrs. Greene work in Bristol Lake?" Agatha asked, her detective instincts suddenly alert.

"I think so? Larissa mentioned once that her mom works for a cleaning company. Not sure which one." Celeste looked at Agatha curiously. "Why?"

"Just curious," Agatha said, but her mind was racing. Catherine Greene had lost her restaurant, her husband, her entire life because of Paul Chambers. If she worked as a house cleaner in Bristol Lake, if she had access to the Crawford house...

"Paul Chambers—that's the man who was murdered, isn't it?" Celeste said, making the connection. "At the tree lighting ceremony?"

"Yes," Agatha said quietly.

"Wow." Celeste sat back. "I mean, I'm not saying Mrs. Greene did anything, but... she had every reason to hate him."

That was an understatement. Catherine Greene had watched her husband die from the stress of losing their family business. She'd had to take on menial work to survive. She'd watched her daughter give up college, give up her dreams.

All because of Paul Chambers.

"I should call Detective Dawson," Agatha said, reaching for her phone. "He should know about this connection."

The phone rang twice before Dawson answered.

"Agatha, I was just about to call you. We've had a development."

Something in his tone made Agatha's stomach tighten. "What kind of development?"

"Catherine Greene just walked into the station twenty minutes ago." Dawson paused. "She confessed to murdering Paul Chambers."

Agatha's breath caught. "She what?"

"She confessed. Voluntarily came in, no lawyer present, and confessed to everything." Dawson's voice was measured, professional. "Said she took the knife from the Crawford house while cleaning—she's been cleaning their house twice a week for the past six months. She kept the knife hidden until the tree lighting ceremony, went to the event, found Paul alone behind the tree stand, and stabbed him. Then she panicked and left the knife beside the body."

"But Rebecca threw the knife in the trash," Agatha said, confused.

"Catherine says she doesn't know anything about that. Maybe Rebecca found the knife later and disposed of it thinking Dennis had done it—we're still sorting out that part. But Catherine has given us every detail about how she planned it, where she hid the knife, how she got Paul alone. She even knew details about the knife that weren't public— the scrollwork on the handle, the specific type of Norwegian silver." Dawson sounded satisfied. "It's a solid confession. Rebecca Crawford will be released within the hour."

"That's..." Agatha struggled to process this. "That's wonderful. For Rebecca, I mean."

"Justice served," Dawson said. "Catherine Greene had

strong motive—Paul destroyed her family's restaurant, her husband died from the stress of it. She had opportunity—she cleaned the Crawford house regularly and had easy access to the knife. And now she's confessed with details only the killer would know. Case closed, Agatha."

"What about Larissa?" Agatha asked. "Catherine's daughter?"

"We've contacted her. She's devastated, as you'd imagine. We'll need her to come in for some follow-up questions, but she's not a suspect. This was Catherine acting alone."

After hanging up, Agatha sat down heavily in a café chair, trying to process what she'd just heard.

"What happened?" Celeste asked, her face pale. "You look shocked."

"Catherine Greene just confessed to murdering Paul Chambers," Agatha said slowly. "She turned herself in to the police."

"Oh my God." Celeste's hands flew to her mouth. "Mrs. Greene? She killed him?"

"Apparently. She gave them all the details." Agatha felt a wave of relief wash over her. "Rebecca Crawford will be released. The real killer is in custody."

"Poor Larissa," Celeste whispered. "First her dad dies, and now her mom's going to prison. That poor girl has lost everything."

Before Agatha could respond, the door burst open and Lorraine swept in, her purple coat billowing dramatically.

"Agatha! Celeste! You will never believe what I have just heard!" Lorraine unwound her scarf with a flourish, her eyes gleaming with the thrill of fresh gossip. "Catherine Greene has confessed to the murder! She walked into the police station and—" She stopped, seeing Agatha's expression. "Ah. You already know."

"Detective Dawson just called," Agatha confirmed.

"Oh." Lorraine looked momentarily deflated, then rallied. "But do you know why she confessed? I have the inside story!"

Agatha's phone buzzed with a text from Emma: *Just heard the news! Coming over now.*

"Emma's on her way," Agatha said. "She'll want to hear this too."

Five minutes later, Emma hurried through the door, breathless and pink-cheeked from the cold. "Is it true? Catherine Greene confessed?"

"It's true," Agatha confirmed. "And Lorraine has details."

"Let me guess," Emma said, settling into a chair and pulling off her gloves. "Lorraine's gossip network strikes again?"

"Mais oui! My friend's cousin knows Lori Crawford—no relation to Dennis, different Crawfords—and Lori is Catherine Greene's cousin." Lorraine sat down with great ceremony. "Lori spoke to the priest's wife just an hour ago, and she said Catherine could not bear to let an innocent woman spend Christmas in jail for something she did!"

"That's... actually very noble of her," Emma said.

"Noble, yes, but also motivated by hatred!" Lorraine leaned forward conspiratorially. "According to Lori, Catherine despised the Crawfords. Dennis and Rebecca treated her terribly, you see. Always looking down on her, making her feel small. 'The help,' they called her. Never said please or thank you. Rebecca would leave passive-aggressive notes about things not being cleaned properly."

"So she framed them deliberately," Agatha said, the pieces clicking into place. "Used their knife to kill Paul, knowing it would point directly to them."

"Exactement! Two birds with one stone—revenge against Paul for destroying her family, and revenge against the Crawfords for treating her like dirt." Lorraine sat back with satisfaction. "Catherine Greene is not just a murderer, she is a very clever murderer. She would have let Rebecca go to trial, let her be convicted, if not for Christmas. Even a killer has some conscience, non?"

"Apparently so," Emma said. She looked at Agatha. "Are you okay? You seem quiet."

"I'm fine," Agatha said. "Just relieved. Rebecca is innocent. Justice has been served. The right person is in custody."

"And we can all have a peaceful Christmas now!" Lorraine declared. "No more investigating, no more suspecting everyone, no more murder talk. Tomorrow we celebrate, oui?"

"Oui," Agatha agreed with a small smile.

Mike stretched and yawned, completely unconcerned with the resolution of the case. He padded over to his food bowl, clearly deciding that if the humans were done with mysteries, it was time for dinner.

"Smart dog," Emma said, laughing. "He has his priorities straight."

They spent the next hour discussing Christmas plans—Lorraine's elaborate dinner menu, Emma's family gathering, Celeste's quiet celebration with her parents. The conversation was light, cheerful, focused on the holiday rather than murder.

By the time Lorraine and Emma left—with promises to

exchange gifts tomorrow—the December sun was setting, painting the snow-covered streets in shades of pink and gold.

Agatha locked up the bookstore and walked home with Mike, enjoying the peaceful evening. Christmas lights glowed in windows. Carols drifted from someone's open door. Bristol Lake looked like a painting, serene and beautiful.

The case was solved. Catherine Greene had confessed, giving details only the killer would know. She'd had motive—Paul destroyed her family. She'd had means—access to the Crawford knife through her cleaning work. She'd had opportunity—she was at the ceremony, anonymous in the crowd.

Everything made sense.

The murder was solved. Rebecca was free. Justice had prevailed.

Agatha should have felt satisfied, triumphant even.

Instead, as she walked up the steps to her light blue house at 93 Knob Hill, she felt... peaceful. Content. Ready to enjoy Christmas without the weight of unsolved mysteries hanging over her.

"Come on, Mike," she said, unlocking her door. "Let's have a quiet evening. We've earned it."

Mike wagged his tail in agreement and trotted inside.

Tomorrow was Christmas. Time to celebrate, not investigate.

The case was closed.

Chapter 27

The Connection

Christmas Eve morning dawned bright and cold, with fresh snow blanketing Bristol Lake overnight. Agatha opened the bookstore, though she didn't expect many customers. Most people were home preparing for the holiday, wrapping last-minute gifts, baking cookies, getting ready for family gatherings.

The case was solved. Catherine Greene had confessed. Rebecca Crawford was free. Justice had been served.

Agatha should have felt content.

Instead, she'd spent half the night lying awake, turning the pieces over in her mind. Something about Catherine's confession nagged at her, though she couldn't quite identify what.

Mike seemed restless too, pacing the bookstore rather than settling by the fireplace as usual. His ears kept swiveling toward the door, as if he were waiting for something—or someone.

"You're as unsettled as I am," Agatha told him, scratching behind his ears. "Though I don't know why."

Emma arrived around ten with a box of Christmas cookies from Eliza's bakery. "Merry Christmas Eve! Eliza sent these over—said they're her gift to you for all the business you send her way."

"That's sweet of her," Agatha said, though she couldn't muster much enthusiasm.

Emma studied her friend's face. "You're still bothered by something."

"I don't know. Maybe I'm just tired." Agatha arranged the cookies on a plate. "Catherine's confession makes perfect sense. She had every reason to kill Paul, and she had access to the knife. Case closed."

"But?" Emma prompted.

"But nothing. I'm overthinking things." Agatha forced a smile. "Let's just enjoy Christmas, okay? No more mysteries."

Around eleven, the door opened and Larissa walked in. Agatha recognized her immediately. But this Larissa looked nothing like the cheerful customer from before. Her face was blotchy and swollen from crying, her eyes red-rimmed, her hands trembling as she unwound her scarf.

"I'm sorry to bother you," Larissa said, her voice shaking. "I just—I needed to get out of the house. I've been at the police station all morning and I couldn't—I can't—" Her voice broke.

"Larissa!" Celeste hurried over from where she'd been restocking shelves. "Oh my God, I heard about your mom. I'm so sorry."

"She confessed," Larissa whispered. "She confessed to murder. My mom. She killed that man and now she's going to prison and it's all my fault."

"How is it your fault?" Agatha asked gently, guiding Larissa to a chair.

"Because Dad died because of Paul Chambers. Because we lost everything. Because Mom has been so sad, so angry, and I should have known—I should have seen—" Larissa dissolved into tears.

Mike, who normally greeted every visitor with enthusiasm, stayed by the fireplace. His ears were back, flat against his head. A low rumble came from his throat—not quite a growl, but close.

Agatha glanced at him, surprised. Mike was friendly with everyone. She'd only seen him react like this a handful of times—with people who'd turned out to be dangerous or untrustworthy.

With people like Paul Chambers.

"Mike, hush," Agatha said quietly, though her detective instincts were suddenly alert.

Celeste sat with Larissa, offering tissues and sympathy. "Your mom must have been in so much pain. Losing your dad, losing the restaurant—"

"She was," Larissa said through her tears. "But I never thought she'd—I mean, murder? My mom?" She looked up at Agatha with desperate eyes. "Do you think she really did it? The police seem convinced, but I just can't believe my mother would kill someone."

"She confessed," Emma said gently. "With details only the killer would know."

"I know, I know. The police told me everything." Larissa wiped her eyes. "About how she took the knife from the Crawford house while cleaning, how she planned it, how she did it during the tree lighting. But it doesn't feel real. None of this feels real."

Mike's rumble grew slightly louder. He was staring at Larissa with an intensity Agatha had rarely seen, his whole body tense.

"Mike, what's wrong with you?" Celeste asked, noticing. "You're being so weird."

"Maybe he senses her distress," Emma suggested. "Dogs can pick up on emotions."

But Agatha wasn't so sure. Mike's reaction wasn't concern or sympathy. It was suspicion. Distrust.

The same way he'd reacted to Paul Chambers at the reception before the tree lighting.

Before Agatha could think more about it, the door burst open with Lorraine's typical dramatic flair. She was wrapped in her purple coat, her hair freshly styled from the salon, and her eyes were gleaming with the excitement of fresh gossip.

"Mes amies! You will never believe what I just heard at the hairdresser!" She stopped short, seeing Larissa's tear-stained face. "Oh. I am interrupting something."

"It's fine," Larissa said, standing and collecting her scarf. "I should go anyway. I just needed—I don't know what I needed. Thank you for listening."

She left quickly, and Mike visibly relaxed once the door closed behind her. He shook himself and padded over to Agatha, pressing against her leg as if seeking reassurance.

"That poor girl," Celeste said. "First her dad, now her mom. It's so awful."

"Oui, très tragique," Lorraine agreed. "But mes amies, I have news! Important news about Catherine Greene!"

"What news?" Agatha asked, her attention sharpening.

"My hairdresser's sister works at the community center—you know, the building next to the town square?" Lorraine settled into a chair, clearly enjoying having crucial information. "She was working the night of the tree lighting, managing the refreshments inside. And she told my hairdresser, who told me, that Catherine Greene was there during the ceremony!"

"At the tree lighting?" Emma asked. "We know she was there—she confessed to being there."

"Non, non, you misunderstand!" Lorraine waved her hands dramatically. "Catherine was inside the community center. During the entire ceremony. From seven o'clock until after eight. The sister remembers specifically because Catherine was so sad, sitting alone in the corner, eating scone after scone. A whole basket of them! The sister was worried about her—said she looked heartbroken, kept crying quietly. She even went over to ask if Catherine was okay, and Catherine said she just needed to be alone for a while."

Agatha's pulse quickened. "During the entire ceremony? Are you sure?"

"The sister is certain! She remembers because she was concerned enough to keep checking on Catherine. The poor woman sat there for over an hour, eating scones and crying. The sister even noted the time because she was worried Catherine might be having some kind of breakdown." Lorraine paused dramatically. "But if Catherine was in the community center eating scones during the tree lighting, then she could not have been behind the tree stand stabbing Paul Chambers, non?"

The words hung in the air.

Emma's eyes widened. "Catherine has an alibi."

"She couldn't have committed the murder," Agatha said slowly, her mind racing. "She was inside the community center, with a witness, during the exact time Paul was killed."

"But she confessed!" Celeste protested. "She gave them all the details—"

"Details she could have learned from someone else," Agatha interrupted. "Details about the knife, about the murder, about how it happened. Details her daughter could have told her."

The pieces were clicking together with horrifying clarity. Catherine Greene hadn't killed Paul Chambers. She'd confessed to protect someone.

To protect Larissa.

Mike's reaction suddenly made perfect sense. He'd sensed what Agatha's conscious mind hadn't yet grasped—that Larissa was dangerous. Untrustworthy. Guilty.

"Mon Dieu," Lorraine breathed. "You think the daughter did it?"

"I think Catherine is protecting her daughter," Agatha said. "Larissa killed Paul Chambers, and when Catherine found out—or maybe she knew all along—she confessed to save her."

"But we don't have proof," Emma said. "Just suspicion and Mike's instincts."

"And an alibi that contradicts Catherine's confession," Agatha added. "Dawson needs to know about this."

She reached for her phone, but Emma stopped her. "Wait. If we're wrong—if Catherine really did do it and just happened to eat scones before or after—we'll look foolish. We need something concrete."

"The video," Celeste said suddenly. "The tourist's video. The one that showed Rebecca throwing away the knife."

"What about it?" Agatha asked.

"The police only released a short clip—the part showing Rebecca. But the tourist was filming for much longer, right? During the ceremony, capturing the crowd and the tree lighting?" Celeste pulled out her phone. "Someone posted the full video online this morning. I saw it on social media. People were commenting about how beautiful the ceremony was, despite what happened."

"Can you find it?" Agatha asked urgently.

Celeste's fingers flew over her phone screen. "Here. Someone uploaded the complete video—almost fifteen minutes long. The police only used about thirty seconds for evidence."

They gathered around Celeste's phone as she hit play. The video started with the crowd gathering, people milling about in winter coats and scarves, the Christmas tree visible in the background. The timestamp showed 7:05 PM.

The video continued—the mayor's speech, children singing carols, the countdown to the tree lighting. The crowd was thick, faces mostly obscured by darkness and winter clothing.

"There," Lorraine pointed. "That is Rebecca, non? At 7:52, throwing something in the trash bin. That is the part the police used."

But Celeste was rewinding, going back to the earlier footage. "I want to see during the actual tree lighting. When Paul was killed."

The timestamp showed 7:20 PM. The crowd was focused on the tree, faces upturned, waiting for the lights.

The camera panned across the gathering, capturing the festive atmosphere.

And then, for just a moment, it caught someone in the crowd—a figure in a dark jacket, moving away from the direction of the tree stand. The footage was grainy, the person's face not visible, but the jacket was distinctive.

"Wait," Celeste said, her voice tight. "Rewind that. Go back five seconds."

Emma took the phone and rewound.

"There. Pause it."

The image froze on the figure in the jacket. It was blurry, taken from behind, but the jacket was clearly visible—dark with the number 19 on the back in white.

"Did you see that?" Celeste whispered.

Chapter 28

The Confrontation

"See what?" Emma asked, squinting at the paused image on Celeste's phone.

"That jacket," Celeste said, her voice shaking slightly. "Number nineteen on the back. That's a cheerleading jacket from Petunia Heights High School."

Agatha leaned closer, studying the blurry figure. The number 19 was clearly visible in white against the dark fabric.

"Lots of people probably have those jackets," Lorraine said, though her tone was doubtful.

"Not lots. The cheerleading squad only makes them for members, and you have to earn your number." Celeste's finger trembled as she pointed at the screen. "Number nineteen. That was Larissa's number. I remember because she was so proud of it—varsity captain her senior year. She wore that jacket everywhere."

"Check the timestamp," Emma said urgently.

Celeste looked. "Seven twenty-three PM."

The exact window when Paul Chambers had been murdered.

"And she's moving away from the tree stand area," Agatha observed. "Walking into the crowd, disappearing into the darkness."

They watched as the figure moved through the frame and vanished. The video continued—the tree lighting, the crowd's applause, the festive celebration—completely unaware that murder had just occurred behind the decorated platform.

"We need to call Detective Dawson," Emma said.

"Non!" Lorraine stood abruptly. "If we call now, we give Larissa time to run. To hide evidence. We should confront her first, get her to confess, then call the police."

"That's dangerous," Emma protested. "She's a murderer—"

"She's a young woman who killed for revenge and is now watching her mother go to prison for her crime," Agatha said quietly. "She must be falling apart. If we approach her carefully, she might confess."

"And if she doesn't?" Emma asked.

"Then we call Dawson immediately and let him handle it." Agatha pulled out her phone. "But Lorraine is right—if we call now, Larissa could run. Or destroy evidence. We need to move quickly."

"I'm coming with you," Lorraine announced.

"Me too," Celeste added.

"No," Agatha said firmly. "Celeste, you need to stay here in case anyone comes looking for us. And Lorraine—"

"Do not even try to tell Lorraine Dubois she cannot come!" Lorraine's eyes flashed. "I have been investigating this case from the beginning! I will not be left behind at the climax!"

Agatha looked at Emma, who shrugged. "Three of us is probably safer than two. And you know Lorraine—she'll just follow us anyway."

"Fine," Agatha conceded. "But everyone stays in the car except Emma and me. Understood?"

"Oui, oui," Lorraine agreed, though her tone suggested she had no intention of following that rule.

Celeste forwarded the video to Agatha's phone. "Be careful. And call me when it's over."

"We will," Agatha promised.

Twenty minutes later, Agatha was driving her 1962 Ford Falcon through the snowy roads toward Petunia Heights, Emma in the passenger seat and Lorraine in the back. Mike sitting alert beside Lorraine, his ears pricked forward.

"Do we have a plan?" Emma asked nervously.

"We tell her we know the truth. We show her the video. We ask her to confess." Agatha's hands were steady on the wheel, but her heart was pounding. "If she refuses, we call Dawson immediately."

"And if she tries to run?"

"She won't get far. Dawson can have officers here in minutes." Agatha turned onto the main road leading to Petunia Heights. "But I don't think she'll run. I think she's been carrying this guilt since the moment she killed Paul. Watching her mother confess must be tearing her apart."

"She should be torn apart," Lorraine said darkly. "She killed a man and let her maman take the blame. This is not the behavior of a good daughter."

"She's young and desperate and destroyed by what Paul did to her family," Agatha said. "That doesn't excuse murder, but it explains it."

The drive to Petunia Heights took twenty minutes through increasingly rural landscape. The town was smaller than Bristol Lake, with a charming main street decorated for Christmas. Agatha followed the GPS to the address Emma had found—a modest apartment building on the edge of town.

"That's her car," Emma said, pointing to a small sedan in the parking lot. "She's home."

Agatha parked and turned to her friends. "Last chance to change your mind."

"Non," Lorraine said firmly. "We finish this."

"Together," Emma agreed.

They climbed out into the cold afternoon air. Mike jumped down and stayed close to Agatha, his body tense and alert. The apartment building was quiet—most people probably out doing last-minute Christmas preparations.

Larissa's apartment was on the second floor. Agatha knocked, her heart hammering.

No answer.

She knocked again. "Larissa? It's Agatha Royale from One Deadly Chapter. I need to talk to you."

A long pause. Then footsteps, slow and reluctant.

The door opened. Larissa stood there in sweatpants and an oversized sweater, her face blotchy from crying. When she saw the three women and the dog, her expression shifted from confusion to wariness.

"What are you doing here?"

"We need to talk," Agatha said gently. "About your mother's confession."

"I already talked to the police. I don't have anything else to say." Larissa started to close the door.

"We know Catherine didn't kill Paul Chambers," Emma said quickly. "We know she has an alibi. She was in the community center eating scones during the murder."

Larissa froze, her hand still on the door.

"We also found video evidence," Agatha continued. "From the tree lighting ceremony. It shows someone in a Petunia Heights cheerleading jacket—number nineteen—walking away from the crime scene at seven twenty-three PM. Right when Paul was killed."

The color drained from Larissa's face.

"Your mother is in jail for a murder she didn't commit," Agatha said quietly. "She's protecting you, Larissa. She confessed to save you. But we know the truth."

For a long moment, Larissa just stared at them. Then her face crumpled and she started to sob—deep, wrenching sobs that shook her entire body.

"I didn't mean for her to confess," Larissa gasped between sobs. "I didn't know she would—I never wanted her to—"

"Let us in," Emma said gently. "Please. Let us help you."

Larissa stepped back, and they filed into the small apartment. It was neat but sparse, with minimal furniture and moving boxes still stacked in corners. The life of someone who'd given up on permanence, on building a future.

Larissa collapsed onto the couch, still crying. Mike stayed near Agatha, watching the young woman with his dark, knowing eyes.

"Tell us what happened," Agatha said, sitting in a chair across from her. "The truth."

Larissa wiped her face with shaking hands. "Paul Chambers destroyed my family. He shut down Villa Toscana with lies and fake violations because we wouldn't pay his bribe. My dad tried to fight it, but nobody believed him. Everyone believed Paul—the respected health inspector with his perfect record."

"Your father died," Emma said softly.

"Six months after we lost the restaurant. Heart attack, they said. But I know the truth—he died of a broken heart. He died because Paul Chambers destroyed something my grandfather built, something my dad poured his whole life into." Larissa's voice was bitter. "And Paul just moved on to his next victim. Didn't even remember our names."

"So you decided to kill him," Lorraine said.

"Not at first. At first I just hated him. Wanted him to suffer the way we'd suffered. But then my mom started cleaning houses to make ends meet, and one of her clients was the Crawfords." Larissa laughed—a harsh, ugly sound. "Dennis and Rebecca Crawford, who treated my mother like dirt. Who left her passive-aggressive notes and never said thank you and looked through her like she was invisible."

"And you saw an opportunity," Agatha said.

"I saw justice." Larissa's eyes were fierce through her tears. "Paul Chambers and the Crawfords—they were both guilty. Paul destroyed families for money, and the Crawfords treated people like my mother as less than human. So I decided to kill two birds with one stone."

"How did you get the knife?" Emma asked.

"My mom always complained about the Crawfords' knife collection—how she had to dust it carefully, how Mrs. Crawford would inspect it and complain if it wasn't perfect. She mentioned the Norwegian silver knife specifically because it was so distinctive." Larissa took a shaky breath. "One day when I was visiting her during her shift—she'd left her phone at home and I brought it to the Crawford house—I saw the knife. Just sitting there in the display cabinet. And I thought... I could use that."

"You stole it," Agatha said.

"I took it. Wrapped it in a towel, hid it in my bag. My mom never even knew. She finished cleaning and we left, and nobody noticed it was gone." Larissa's voice dropped. "I kept it hidden for two weeks, planning. The tree lighting ceremony was perfect—big crowd, everyone distracted, Paul would be there judging. I could do it and disappear into the crowd and nobody would know."

"But you wore your cheerleading jacket," Emma pointed out.

"It was cold! And dark. I didn't think anyone would notice the number, would recognize it." Larissa wiped her eyes. "I went to the ceremony, waited for my chance. When Paul stepped away from the other judges, I followed him. Told him I had information about his... consulting fees. That I knew about the bribes he'd been taking, and I wanted to discuss terms."

"He followed you because he was worried you'd expose him," Emma said.

"Exactly. He got this look on his face—nervous, angry. He grabbed my arm and said we needed to talk somewhere private, away from the crowd." Larissa's voice dropped. "He led me behind the tree stand himself. That's when I told him who I really was—Larissa Greene, Anthony Greene's daughter. I wanted him to know why he was dying. But I don't think he even remembered Villa Toscana. He looked confused, like he couldn't place which restaurant out of all the ones he'd destroyed."

"And then you stabbed him," Lorraine said bluntly.

"And then I stabbed him," Larissa whispered. "I told him who I was—Larissa Greene, Anthony Greene's daughter. I wanted him to know why he was dying. But I don't think he even remembered Villa Toscana. He looked confused, like he couldn't place which restaurant out of all the ones he'd destroyed."

Agatha felt a chill. Paul Chambers had ruined so many lives that he couldn't even remember individual families.

"What did you do after?" Emma asked.

"I panicked. I dropped the knife beside him and ran. Got back into the crowd, tried to act normal, waited for the tree lighting like nothing had happened." Larissa's hands were shaking. "I thought I'd gotten away with it. The knife would point to the Crawfords—their knife, their grudge against Paul. Perfect frame."

"But then Dennis found the body first," Agatha said.

"I didn't know that. Didn't know Rebecca had thrown the knife away. I just knew that days passed and then Rebecca got arrested and I thought—" Larissa's voice broke. "I thought it worked. I thought justice was served. Paul was dead, the

Crawfords would pay for how they treated people like my mother, and I could finally breathe again."

"But your mother figured it out," Emma guessed.

"She saw the news about Rebecca's arrest. Saw which knife was used. Knew I'd been to the Crawford house that day." Larissa sobbed harder. "She confronted me yesterday. Asked me point-blank if I'd killed Paul. And I couldn't lie to her. I broke down and told her everything."

"And she went to the police and confessed," Agatha said quietly.

"She said she couldn't let an innocent woman go to prison. That she'd already lost my father and our restaurant, but she wouldn't lose me too. She'd confess, say she did it, and I'd be free." Larissa looked up with red, swollen eyes. "But I can't let her do that. I can't let my mother go to prison for something I did. That's not justice. That's just more destruction."

"How can we prove you're telling the truth?" Agatha asked gently. "That you're not just confessing to free your mother, the way she confessed to protect you?"

Larissa hesitated, then stood and went to her bedroom. She returned with a small evidence bag—the kind used for protecting items. Inside was a cell phone.

"I took his phone. I thought there might be evidence of his corruption on it, proof of the bribes and threats. I was going to turn it in anonymously later, make sure people knew what kind of man Paul really was." She handed it to Agatha. "But I never got the chance. And now..."

"Now we need to call Detective Dawson," Agatha said gently.

Larissa nodded, resigned. "I know. I'm ready. I can't keep running from this."

AGATHA MADE THE CALL, and Dawson arrived thirty minutes later with two officers. He listened to Larissa's confession, read her her rights, and placed her under arrest with a gentleness that suggested he understood the tragedy of it all.

"Catherine Greene will be released immediately," Dawson told them as the officers led Larissa out to the police car. "And Rebecca Crawford's name will be fully cleared. You did good work, Agatha. All of you."

As they watched the police car drive away, Lorraine sighed heavily. "This is so sad. A young woman, her whole life ruined. For what? Revenge? It solves nothing."

"Paul destroyed her family," Emma said. "I'm not saying what she did was right, but I understand it."

"Understanding and condoning are different things," Agatha said. She felt exhausted, drained by the investigation and its conclusion. "Larissa made a choice. Now she'll face the consequences."

Mike pressed against her leg, offering comfort.

"At least Catherine is free," Emma said. "And Rebecca. Two innocent women who don't have to pay for someone else's crime."

"Oui," Lorraine agreed. "That is something. Not everything, but something."

The drive back to Bristol Lake was quiet, each of them lost in thought. The winter landscape passed by—snow-covered fields, houses decorated for Christmas, the occasional church steeple rising against the gray sky.

By the time they reached Bristol Lake, it was late afternoon. Christmas Eve was settling over the town like a blessing, lights beginning to glow in windows, the promise of celebration in the air.

Agatha dropped Emma and Lorraine at their homes with promises to see them tomorrow for Christmas dinner. Then she drove home with Mike, parked her Ford Falcon in the driveway, and walked into her house.

She called Dawson from her kitchen. "Is Catherine released yet?"

"Just finished the paperwork. She's on her way home." Dawson paused. "She wanted me to thank you. Said you saved her from making the biggest mistake of her life—letting her daughter's guilt destroy them both."

"I'm glad we figured it out in time," Agatha said.

"Merry Christmas, Agatha."

"Merry Christmas, Detective."

After hanging up, Agatha walked to her desk where her Royal KMM sat waiting. She rolled in a fresh sheet of paper and typed a single line:

Chapter 29

Epilogue

Christmas morning dawned clear and bright over Bristol Lake, the fresh snow sparkling like diamonds in the winter sun. Agatha woke early, Mike already awake and wagging his tail with the excitement that only Christmas could inspire in a dog who had no concept of holidays but understood that something special was happening.

"Merry Christmas, boy," Agatha said, scratching behind his ears. He responded by doing a little dance on his hind legs, something he only did when he was exceptionally happy.

By nine o'clock, Agatha had opened One Deadly Chapter—not for business, but because word had spread that she'd be there for a few hours on Christmas morning, and Bristol Lake had a tradition of neighbors stopping by shops to wish each other well.

The bookstore looked magical. White lights twinkled throughout, garlands draped every shelf, and the small tree in the café corner glowed with warmth. Eliza had sent over fresh cinnamon rolls and Christmas cookies, and Agatha had coffee brewing.

The first visitor was Gladys, arriving at 9:15 with a plate of her famous fudge. "Merry Christmas, dear! I wanted to thank you for everything you did. Rebecca Crawford stopped by my house yesterday—she's finally free, and her Christmas won't be spent in jail. You gave that woman her life back."

"I just found the truth," Agatha said, accepting the fudge with genuine pleasure. "But thank you, Gladys. Merry Christmas."

"Book club in the new year?" Gladys asked with a twinkle in her eye.

"Absolutely. And no more real-life mysteries—just the fictional kind."

"Thank goodness for that!"

Celeste arrived next, bundled in a bright red coat and carrying a gift bag. "Merry Christmas! I got you something— it's not much, but I wanted to thank you for letting me be part of solving the case. That was the most exciting thing that's ever happened to me!"

Inside the bag was a beautiful bookmark with a quote from Agatha Christie: "The impossible could not have happened, therefore the impossible must be possible in spite of appearances."

"It's perfect," Agatha said, genuinely touched. "Thank you, Celeste."

Over the next hour, a steady stream of townspeople stopped by. Eliza delivered more cookies "because Christmas requires excessive amounts of cookies, non-negotiable."

"I just saw Rebecca and Dennis," Eliza said, arranging the cookie tins. "They're spending a quiet Christmas together, talking about renewing their vows. Can you imagine? Almost losing each other made them realize what they have."

"That's wonderful," Agatha said. "And Catherine Greene?"

"Home with her family. Poor woman will support Larissa through the trial, but at least they're together." Eliza hugged her warmly. "Merry Christmas, dear."

Raymond Aguilar arrived with a bottle of wine and his characteristic quiet smile. "Congratulations on solving another case, Agatha. Bristol Lake can be proud."

"Thank you, Raymond. Though I wish the circumstances had been different."

"Don't we all." He settled into one of the café chairs for a moment. "At least the tree lighting wasn't a complete disaster. Rockland took first place in the competition, but we placed a respectable second. Given everything that happened, I'd call that a victory."

"I'd call it a miracle we placed at all."

"Resilience," Raymond said simply. "This town has it in spades. Always has." He stood, preparing to leave. "Will you be at the New Year's gathering at City Hall?"

"Wouldn't miss it."

"Good. We'll need people like you there—people who care about this community." He paused at the door. "Merry Christmas, Agatha."

After the visitors tapered off, Mike barked happily and ran to the door where Emma and Lorraine were arriving together, both laden with bags and packages.

"Joyeux Noël!" Lorraine sang out, sweeping in with her usual dramatic flair. She wore a spectacular red coat with what appeared to be actual jingle bells sewn onto it. "Lorraine has brought contributions to Christmas dinner! Wine, cheese, and French pastries that are magnifique!"

"I brought side dishes," Emma said more practically, setting her bags on the café table. "And presents! We're doing presents, right?"

"After dinner," Agatha said with a smile. "But first, I think we should close up here and head to my house. Christmas dinner doesn't cook itself."

They walked together through the snowy streets of Bristol Lake, past houses decorated with lights and wreaths, past the town square where the Christmas tree still glowed. A group of children were building a snowman near the gazebo, their laughter carrying on the cold air.

"It's beautiful, non?" Lorraine said, looking around with satisfaction. "Bristol Lake at Christmas. Like a storybook."

"Or a mystery novel," Emma added with a grin.

"No more mysteries!" Agatha protested. "At least not until the new year."

At home, they cooked together—Agatha managing the turkey, Emma preparing sweet potatoes and green beans, Lorraine creating what she called "a traditional French Christmas salad" that involved more cheese than lettuce. Mike supervised from his spot by the kitchen door, hoping for dropped food and occasionally receiving small treats "because it's Christmas and even dogs deserve celebration!"

By three o'clock, the table was set with Agatha's best dishes—inherited from her stepmother Joanne, the woman who'd left her this house and the bookstore and, inadvertently, a whole new life. The food was arranged beautifully: golden turkey, creamy mashed potatoes, honey-glazed carrots,

Emma's sweet potato casserole with marshmallow topping, Lorraine's cheese-laden salad, fresh rolls, cranberry sauce.

"It's a feast!" Emma declared.

"It's perfect," Agatha agreed.

They were just sitting down when someone knocked at the door. Mike barked and ran to investigate, tail wagging furiously.

"Who could that be?" Lorraine wondered.

Agatha opened the door to find Detective Dawson standing on her porch with a pie in his hands, looking slightly sheepish.

"I hope I'm not intruding. I was going to be alone today, and I thought—well, I brought apple pie. Made it myself, though I can't promise it's any good."

"You're not intruding at all," Agatha said warmly, stepping aside. "Come in. We have more than enough food."

"And wine!" Lorraine called out. "Come, Detective! Christmas is for friends, and we are all friends here!"

They set another place, and Dawson joined them at the table. For a moment, they all just looked at each other—this unlikely group thrown together by murder and mystery, now gathered for Christmas dinner.

"Should we say grace?" Emma suggested.

"I will!" Lorraine announced. She clasped her hands together dramatically. "Thank you for this food, for this friendship, for solving murders together without getting killed ourselves, and for Eliza's cookies. Amen!"

"That's not exactly traditional," Emma said, laughing.

"It is Lorraine's tradition! And it is perfect!"

They ate and talked and laughed. The conversation flowed easily—memories of the case now that it was safely solved, stories from past Christmases, plans for the new year. Dawson told them about his previous job in a bigger city, why he'd moved to Bristol Lake seeking peace. Emma talked about her dreams of maybe writing a mystery novel someday. Lorraine regaled them with increasingly dramatic stories about her time in New Orleans, where she'd acquired her French identity after a concussion at Saint Charles Street.

Mike circulated under the table, receiving "accidental" dropped food from everyone.

After dinner, they moved to the living room where Agatha's small Christmas tree glowed in the corner. They exchanged gifts—practical things like books and scarves, but given with love. Lorraine gave everyone festive berets "because we must all look French together!" Emma had found a vintage typewriter key necklace for Agatha. Dawson sheepishly presented Agatha with a magnifying glass "for your detective work—since we both know you'll be investigating again eventually."

As evening fell, carolers came down Knob Hill, their voices bright and clear in the cold air. They gathered on Agatha's porch and sang "Silent Night" and "O Holy Night" and "We Wish You a Merry Christmas."

The five of them—Agatha, Emma, Lorraine, Dawson, and Mike—stood at the window watching the carolers, watching the snow begin to fall again.

"This is nice," Emma said quietly. "Being together like this."

"It is better than nice," Lorraine declared. "It is magnifique! This is what Christmas is supposed to be—good food, good friends, good wine, and no one trying to kill anyone!"

"Setting the bar pretty low there," Dawson said with a smile.

"After the year we've had? Low bar is good bar!"

Agatha looked around her living room—at her friends laughing and talking, at Mike sprawled contentedly by the fireplace, at the Christmas tree with its vintage ornaments. This house had become a home. This town had become her community. And these people had become her family.

Lorraine raised her wine glass. "A toast! To Agatha Royale, solver of mysteries and collector of friends! To Bristol Lake! And to Christmas!"

They clinked glasses, and drank to friendship, to justice, to new beginnings.

"Merry Christmas, everyone," Agatha said softly.

"Merry Christmas," they echoed back.

Outside, the carolers moved on to the next house, their voices fading into the snowy night.

Eliza's Christmas Gingerbread Cookies

Ingredients:

- 3 cups all-purpose flour
- 1 ½ teaspoons baking powder
- ¾ teaspoon baking soda
- ¼ teaspoon salt
- 1 tablespoon ground ginger
- 1 ¾ teaspoons ground cinnamon
- ¼ teaspoon ground cloves
- 6 tablespoons unsalted butter, softened
- ¾ cup packed dark brown sugar
- 1 large egg
- ½ cup molasses
- 2 teaspoons vanilla extract

Instructions:

1. Sift together flour, baking powder, baking soda, salt, and spices.

2. Beat butter and brown sugar until fluffy. Add egg, molasses, and vanilla.
3. Gradually add dry ingredients until dough forms.
4. Chill dough 1 hour.
5. Roll out and cut into festive shapes.
6. Bake at 350°F for 8-10 minutes.
7. Decorate with royal icing once cooled.

Emma's Sweet Potato Casserole

Ingredients:

- 4 cups mashed sweet potatoes
- ½ cup sugar
- 2 eggs
- ⅓ cup milk
- ¼ cup butter, melted
- 1 teaspoon vanilla

Topping:

- 1 cup brown sugar
- ½ cup flour
- ⅓ cup butter, melted
- 1 cup chopped pecans
- 2 cups mini marshmallows

Instructions:

1. Mix sweet potatoes, sugar, eggs, milk, butter, and vanilla.
2. Pour into greased 9x13 pan.
3. Mix topping ingredients (except marshmallows) and sprinkle over potatoes.
4. Bake at 350°F for 25 minutes.
5. Add marshmallows and bake 10 more minutes until golden.

Also by Ella Andrew

The Agatha Royale Mystery Series

- One Deadly Chapter
- One Deadly Batch
- One Deadly Needle
- One Deadly Safari
- One Deadly manuscript (coming Soon)
- One Deadly Premiere (coming Soon)

The Ashford Creek Mysteries

Quick reads perfect for your lunch break or evening escape

- Death at the Teacup Inn
- Death at the Sweet Festival
- Death by Recipe
- Death at the Halloween Vigil
- Death at Rosemary Cottage
- Death at the Friendsgiving Table

Each Ashford Creek Mystery is a complete story you can enjoy in about 2 hours.

All books available on Amazon